To Breathe

Also by Antonia Hildebrand and published by Ginninderra Press
The Blind Colossus

Antonia Hildebrand

To Breathe
& other stories

To Breathe & other stories
ISBN 978 1 76041 160 2
Copyright © Antonia Hildebrand 2016
Cover design: Maryann Hine

First published 2016 by
Ginninderra Press
PO Box 3461 Port Adelaide 5015
www.ginninderrapress.com.au

Contents

Foreword

To Breathe is a challenging book of great relevance in a world where each day the media gives accounts of domestic violence and personal tragedies. It is good to have a writer of insight and compassion reveal what lies behind such events.

In these eighteen stories, Hildebrand explores the darker side of life. From the opening lines of the first story, 'Bone Cold Day', where we watch a headless chicken running round and round the yard, blood spurting, we know that we are entering a world of savagery and bloodshed, and the undercurrent of violence that is established in this story prevails throughout this remarkable collection.

The everyday world is not as simple as it seems. The apparently harmless 'Sewing Circle' becomes the vehicle for four tales of exploitation and troubled relationships as four seemingly ordinary women tell their stories. Even the relationship between ladies organising flowers in the church is revealed as based on hostility, contempt and betrayal. But the majority of stories are far more explicit in their exploration of domestic violence, drug addiction and abusive family relationships, while the aptly titled 'In Extremis' takes readers directly into a situation of abduction, rape and torture.

Elements of the supernatural further darken the picture, and we are left unsure whether what we see in 'Objectivity' is really the transformation of scientist into monkey or simply the product of the diseased imagination of his offsider. The world of the future in 'The Settlement' shows us a 2032 where drug addicts are confined to die in miserable conditions. A simple Queensland holiday for two sisters in 'Roads and Cliffs' is permeated with fear and tension, and the sense of lurking violence is found in even the most prosaic situations.

Hildebrand's skill in evoking these scenes is the product of the sensitivity which makes her a fine poet: the opening lines of 'Fish' remind us that

> Memories are strange things. Slippery, like fish escaping a net, and they deceive us if they can. Make us long for things that never were – or never were the way we remember them.

When Kerry's children are taken away by Social Services from their drug addict mother in 'Slipstream', she listens to her daughter screaming, but is unable to respond.

> Instead, she floated silently in the drug's slipstream, like a scientific specimen in a jar of ethanol. As cold and distant as a star in a crisp, dark winter sky. As lost as paradise.

It is reassuring to find the occasional moments of affirmation: a mother looks at her son as they return home:

> 'You're quiet. What are you thinking?'
> 'Nothing. I'm waiting to see the pyramid. It's one of the Seven Wonders of the World, you know.'
> I looked at his smooth dark head and his serious brown eyes.
> 'And love is the eighth,' I told him.
> He didn't sneer and he didn't look embarrassed, he just nodded. All children know that this is true. I had forgotten it until that moment.

But these moments are rare; the prevailing feeling is that of the end of 'Waiting for the Storm':

> I remember the feeling I had – that there was no safety anywhere; inside the house or out. In a way, I suppose I've never lost that feeling.

These are important stories, because they give us imaginative insight into lives that, for most of us, are known only through newspaper and television accounts. It is a world that is relevant and significant, and we need to understand it. This powerful collection will not leave a reader untouched.

Valerie Volk

Bone-cold Day

The chicken ran round and round the yard, blood spurting. It had no head.

Watching it, Roma went white to the lips. It had been so many years but she was never likely to forget. Whenever she thought of that winter's day so long ago, there were feelings of regret and feelings of grief but she remembered too that when it happened there had been a feeling almost of relief because she had known, deep down, that it was going to happen.

She had married John Soames because she was in love with him. He was five years younger than her and he had a reputation as a bit of a wild man. He had rarely shown her the temper he was well known for, the temper that went with his red hair and an Irish ancestor in the shape of a great-grandfather also named John Soames. The story went that he'd been hanged for murder. A drunken fight on a back road in County Cork had turned into a charge of murder. His wife emigrated to Australia to escape the disgrace, taking her two sons with her.

More important to Roma than any family history was the fact that John Soames seemed to like and accept her son Jimmy, five years old when they married. Jimmy was the product of a casual affair that had only lasted two months. No deep feelings on either side. Jimmy's father was a carpenter, a traveller who couldn't stop travelling. He never stayed anywhere long and he blamed this on the fact that one of his ancestors had been a Viking warrior who'd raped and pillaged his way through the world aboard a longship. Stephen Palmstad, Jimmy's father, was blond, blue eyed and beautiful and so was his son. Jimmy was an angelic-looking child with a sweet and affectionate nature.

John Soames was not good-looking but he had a strange, powerful face, long and pointed like a fox's and a magnetism that drew people to him. It drew Roma to him too. Later she shuddered to remember it. Later she thought of him as the spider and herself as the fly and she thought of Jimmy as someone who watched the spider catch the fly and didn't know what he saw. She turned twenty-seven the day after the wedding and she could still remember thinking that she was like a boat anchoring in a safe harbour after what had been a fairly turbulent voyage.

Roy caught the chicken by the legs and held it upside down. It flapped its wings and the blood dripped from it on to the dusty ground. It twitched a few more times and then was still. There were tears in Roma's eyes and she turned away.

'Nice big bird and not too old either. You can do mashed potato and beans and I'll pick some of that new corn,' Roy said.

He was a big man, tanned and fit. He'd been a farmer all his life and he had pale blue eyes and silver hair that had once been jet black, razor-cut short all over his head. He had brought her back from the brink of madness and taught her to trust again. He'd given her four daughters, all grown and married themselves now and he was like a part of her after all these years. He couldn't take away the past, though. No one could do that.

How had it started? Hard to recall the beginning of something that had begun so subtly, so long ago. She remembered a day in Queen's Park. Jimmy on the swing and John Soames pushing him.

'Higher,' Jimmy had shouted. 'Higher.'

So John had pushed him higher and higher and then still higher until Jimmy was screaming with terror and Roma had run across the park on that perfect day of spring sunshine and bird calls and grabbed John by the shoulders.

'Stop it!' she shouted. 'Can't you see he's scared?'

John Soames laughed and turned on her the face of a thug, a schoolyard bully. 'He's okay,' he said.

Other people were now watching the screaming child and the man who wouldn't stop pushing him higher and higher. He only stopped because a man who turned out to be an off-duty policeman came over.

'He's had enough, mate,' he said. 'You better stop now.'

Roma could still hear the voice the man had used. He was used to dealing with emotional cripples. Burning with shame, she realised that that was what the man she had married was.

Even when he stopped pushing, he held the swing so high that Jimmy's feet couldn't quite touch the ground, watching him cry hysterically, the way boys watch bees burning under a magnifying glass. Finally Roma pushed past him and snatched her son off the swing.

'Calm down, for Christ's sake. No big deal,' he said. Then he flopped down on the tartan picnic rug and lit a cigarette. His face was serene and untroubled. No sense of wrongdoing showed in his eyes.

Roma comforted her distressed child and felt the sensation she remembered from going down in a lift – dropping in an emotional free fall. She was almost sure that was the first time. That was how it started.

'I'll have to pluck the bloody thing now,' Roy was saying. Giving her a rueful grin. 'Bugger of a job. Make us a cup of tea, love.' He sighed and sat down on a low stool with a large pot of boiling water at his feet.

Roma went into the house and put the big, battered kettle over the flame of the wood stove. Reaching up on top of the kitchen cupboards, she brought down a dusty photo album. On the first page was a photo of her and John Soames with Jimmy in the middle.

Jimmy was about six and already he was cringing away from John Soames and holding his mother's hand as if he was afraid to let go. Looking at the photo, she asked herself why. As she had so many times over the years. Why hadn't she gone? Why hadn't she got Jimmy out of that house and away from John Soames? The answer – pathetic after all these years and what they'd taught her – was that she was still in love with Soames. He had a powerful sexual attraction for her. He also owned two farms and she believed that he could give her what she'd always wanted out of life – a man she loved and financial security. Hypnotised by this fantasy, like a rabbit caught in blinding light, she went on trying to make it work. Trying to believe it was her dream come true, in the face of all the evidence to the contrary.

She turned the page. A photo taken at a barbecue. She went cold remembering that night. She was having a good time, sipping wine, laughing and talking. Glad to get out of the house; glad to see Jimmy playing with the other kids and enjoying himself. The warning signs were all there but she ignored them the way she ignored all the things she should have been paying attention to.

John Soames was drinking heavily, always a sign of anger or unhappiness with him. He was glaring at her and he was snapping at Jimmy but he controlled himself until they got back to the farm. Then, as soon as they were in the door – the car keys were still in her hand, she remembered – he backhanded her across the face and she fell sideways and slid across the polished wood floor. Jimmy started crying with fear and John Soames grabbed him by the collar and shook him the way a dog shakes a rat.

Jimmy was screaming and holding his hands out to her. 'Mummy,' he screamed, 'make him stop!'

Dazed and uncomprehending, she got to her feet. 'Stop it!' she shouted. 'John, stop it!'

She started to cry and he dropped Jimmy and grabbed her by the hair. 'Had a good time, did you? Ignoring me all night. Talking to Graham Roberts. I saw you. Think I'm blind or something?'

'Who?' she could hear herself babbling, couldn't stop. 'What do you mean?'

Jimmy ran over and hid behind her.

'Who? What?' John mocked. 'Don't give me that bullshit!'

She swallowed, steeled herself. 'Look, you're drunk,' she said firmly. 'Go to bed.' She sounded calm, though she felt anything but calm.

He stared at her for a while, then, surprisingly, he turned round and walked away up the hall.

She stood in the silent house, holding her son to her, afraid to move until she heard Soames snoring. Then she picked Jimmy up and let him burrow into her neck. He was gasping with holding in sobs he was too frightened to cry. He made muffled little fear sounds while Roma felt the same shattered, shocked feeling she remembered from a car crash when she was sixteen. It all seemed unreal. She knew now that that was the night she should have left. Instead, she told herself that he was drunk, that he didn't know what he was doing. She held Jimmy and dried his eyes and told herself that tomorrow was another day.

The next day John Soames left a box of chocolates on the kitchen table. Not wrapped. No card. No apology.

The piercing shriek of the boiling kettle went through her and made her jump as if she'd been shot. She made the tea and put some biscuits on a plate. She put the photo album back on top of the cupboard. When she carried the tray outside into the bright, dry autumn sunshine, Roy looked up from the half-plucked chicken.

'Thanks, love,' he said. 'You all right?'

She could never hide anything from Roy. That rough exterior hid a sensitivity that was almost intuition.

'Just thinking, that's all,' she said.

'Umm,' he said, sipping his tea.

He knew when to leave her alone too. The product of twenty years of cohabitation. Then she thought, No, he's always been like that. He just knows.

She didn't want to but she started thinking about that last winter. She would always think about it. That was her punishment. It was the winter Jimmy turned eight; the winter they moved to the old farm; the one where Soames had grown up.

The big farm, 'Wyreema', was left in the care of a manager, a man with five unruly children and a wife who'd looked Roma over with a sour look. As if she'd swallowed a bucket of lemons, Roma thought. The old farm, 'Brookfield', was a run-down place near Dalby where they ran a herd of dairy cattle. Foxes had killed the black hens they'd brought with them.

There were frosts every morning and she miscarried a baby soon after they got there, the summer before.

Soames wasn't responsible, though her pregnancy hadn't made him any less free with his fists or his abusive language. She thought now that she had made herself lose the baby because she wanted to punish him and because she couldn't inflict him on another child. She'd cried her eyes out and fallen into black despair but looking back from where she was now, she thought how good it was that she hadn't had that baby.

The day it happened was fiercely cold and windy but a day of bright sunshine. Soames woke up angry and he stayed that way. In fact, he got angrier as the day went on. By the time he came in for lunch, he was irrational with anger. She'd seen him this way before and she thought that if she kept out of his way and told Jimmy to stay in his room, it would blow over, but there was no placating him.

It was three o'clock (she heard it on the radio, which was on in the kitchen) when it all began to go wrong. He'd come up from the dairy at half past two. For him to eat that late wasn't unusual but he got a beer out of the fridge, and that was.

'Look at this place!' he suddenly burst out after the third beer. 'Look at it! I work like a dog and look how I have to live!'

'I'm sorting out some summer clothes to give the Simmonses for their boys. I have some Jimmy's grown out of,' Roma said, beginning to feel that sick feeling in her stomach. He never drank in the daytime. 'I'll clean it up when I'm finished.'

'That little shit!' he yelled at the mention of Jimmy. 'He's not even my kid. I work my fingers to the bone and he looks at me as if I'm Attila the Hun.' He wiped his mouth with the back of his hand and put the bottle to his lips again.

Roma felt the blood draining out of her face and her heart speeding up. Whatever was wrong was not going to go away. I'll listen to him, she thought. Let him talk and I won't say a thing.

By four she decided she would move the rifle from where he kept it in the downstairs laundry. She still only thought of it as a precaution. She put it in the linen press.

'A man'ud be better off dead,' he was saying. 'Better off dead.'

She knew now, looking back down the distance of the years, that this had been coming for a long time. Probably all his life. Later she found out that one of his brothers had committed suicide and an uncle had died in an asylum.

'Runs in the family,' his rough, leather-faced old mother had told her much later. Too late.

If she'd known, she could have faced facts and she would have, wouldn't she? Stopped blaming herself and the fact that she had Jimmy and seen that Soames was the problem? Even now she didn't know the answer. What did it matter? No one had told her.

By five he was prowling around the house looking for the gun. 'Where is it? You've taken it, haven't you? Give it to me,' he roared and then he went up the hall and threw open the door to Jimmy's room. He dragged him out; Jimmy was white with terror. Too scared even to cry.

Almost casually, Soames produced a small but extremely sharp knife he always had in his coat pocket. 'Give me the gun or I'll kill him,' he said, holding the knife against Jimmy's throat.

Dry-mouthed, unable to catch her breath, unable to think, she stared at the knife. Then she ran to the linen press to get the rifle. If she gave it to him, he would kill them all, she knew that.

When she got back with the gun, Soames had dragged Jimmy out on to the veranda.

'Give me the rifle, you bitch,' he raved. 'Give me my gun.'

She faced him on the veranda with the rifle. Desperate, she realised he would never back down. Not when he was like this.

'Let him go,' she said, in a voice that shook.

'Bitch!' he roared, his normally pale face red with rage. 'Give me the gun,' he said, then glanced at Jimmy. 'You don't love me, do you?'

If she'd been able to convince him that she loved him, half-mad with terror as she was at that moment, would it have made any difference? She looked at him; she was bewildered but still hopeful, tears in her eyes. 'Let him go,' she pleaded, pointing the rifle at him.

'Okay,' he said with a mad twitch of his shoulders. 'I'll let him go.'

Then with one swift, slashing movement he brought the knife across the child's throat and pushed him away. The boy put his hands up to his throat and tried to run, stumbling down the stairs. He ran in staggering circles in the dusty yard, blood running between his fingers. Then he fell and was still.

Someone was screaming. She realised it was her. Briefly she met Soames's mad, triumphant gaze and then she aimed the rifle at him and pulled the trigger over and over again until it was empty.

They told her this later. She had no memory of doing it. She only remembered carrying Jimmy up into the house, a wax doll in her arms. He died in the kitchen. The radio said it was 5.45 p.m. She whispered to Jimmy that no one would ever be able to hurt him again. This comfort, so hard and bitter that she thought it would stop her heart, was all she had and if she hadn't hung on to it, she would have reloaded the gun and blown her brains out.

The sky was pitch black and the radio told her it was 6.30 p.m. when the police car pulled up near the veranda. They told her she'd phoned them. She couldn't remember. She heard the siren scream up to the house and suddenly stop, choked off. They found her in the kitchen, lying in a pool of blood with Jimmy still in her arms.

'My husband's dead,' was all she said before they pulled Jimmy out of her arms and took him away.

A court hearing cleared her of any blame but she knew better.

'Have a biscuit, love,' Roy said. 'Go on.'

'No, Roy. I'm not hungry.'

'Come on, old girl. You've got all of this to eat yet,' pointing at the chicken.

She shook her head and he put his arms around her. She leaned her head on his shoulder. Looking up into the blue infinity of the sky, she watched a small cloud chase other clouds. It was like watching a child at play.

Death of an Enemy

The Middle East, they called it, as if it was some kind of middle way. It seemed to indicate a place where moderation could be expected. Harry Coates brooded on this over his breakfast egg and two pieces of burned toast.

Radio National, June 2001: 'Today in the Middle East a suicide bomber has carried out an attack on Tel Aviv nightclub. Most of the dead were young people enjoying a night out at the popular nightspot.'

Harry now had his head in the newspaper but out of the corner of his eye he saw that stupid bastard Jeff Dark climb the fence and stroll into his yard. Dark made himself comfortable – opened his own newspaper – and settled on one of the white plastic garden chairs in Coates's backyard. Rage flooded Coates' brain. He felt the heat burn slowly up to the top of his head and he jumped up from the kitchen table. The remaining piece of burnt toast flew into the air and landed buttered side down on the floor.

The Coateses had moved to Brisbane, to this stucco house, in 1949 and had lived there ever since. He walked to the back door and threw it open. A cup fell off the hutch his wife had bought two years before she died and smashed to bits.

'You!' Coates roared. 'Dark! I know you can hear me! Get out of my yard!'

Dark smiled and slowly, very slowly folded his paper. At glacial pace he stood up and turned to smirk at Coates. Then at a very leisurely pace he walked up the drive at the side of the house and out the front gate.

Dark had moved in six months ago. Too late Coates had realised that the man was crazy. Dark had been released from jail a month before he bought the house. Wrongfully convicted of a murder and imprisoned for twelve years until DNA evidence proved that he hadn't committed the crime. He was paid compensation and his conviction was quashed but it was too late for Jeff Dark. Twelve years of brutality had done something to his mind. He would never be the man he was when he went into jail. A couple of horrific bashings and a suicide attempt had seen to that. Dark was now a misfit. Sometimes Coates had the impression of an imp trapped in a fifty-year-old body. Some days the man seemed almost normal. Other days he wandered like a child into Coates's yard as if searching for the home he would never go back to. His wife had divorced him soon after the guilty verdict.

At first, Coates had tried to reason with him. 'Don't climb the fence. Look what you've done to my roses,' he told him, looking at the long, bloody scratches on Dark's legs.

Dark seemed unaware of the scratches and smiled his empty, angelic smile. He looked at Coates and said slyly, 'I could cut your throat, you know. When you were sleeping.'

Coates felt the blood drain from his face. 'What?' he said. 'What did you say?' Coates was no coward. He had fought at Tobruk in the Second World War and been decorated – but this was something quite different. This was something he couldn't understand; something he couldn't fight. Calls to the police went unheeded.

'What's he done?' the police would say.

'He's in my yard. He's on my land. He's invading…' – how he hated the newspeak he was forced to resort to, to explain his situation – 'invading my space."

The policeman had a very young voice and Coates thought he sounded amused. 'Space Invaders, eh?' he said.

'Look, are you taking this seriously?' Coates demanded, quite unnecessarily, since the answer was obvious.

'Of course I am, sir,' the young voice said, 'but unless he does something…'

'He doesn't do anything! He's not stupid enough to do anything. He sits in my yard. On my land. He's trespassing, isn't that enough?'

'We'll have a word with him. Your address ,sir? And your neighbour's address?"

But nothing was ever done. A few times, Coates saw policemen having a polite conversation with Dark on his front porch; but with the cunning of the mad, Dark was perfectly reasonable. He lied of course. What else could he do? The police may not even have believed him but they couldn't afford to be seen to be harassing a man who had been wrongly convicted and imprisoned.

They gave Coates a funny look when they caught him spying on them from his kitchen window. After that it was hopeless. The police always took Dark's side. They decided Coates was persecuting Dark and future phone calls to the police met with cold politeness and the patient tone one took with nutters.

One day while Coates was digging some manure in around the roses, Dark's mad face appeared at the top of the fence. 'They say you're terrorising me. I suppose that means you're a terrorist.' He smiled his blank smile and looked at Coates curiously as if expecting an answer. 'I'm a victim of injustice,' he added before disappearing.

Coates was so enraged he threw his spade and heard it hit the side of the shed. He felt dizzy. His chest hurt as if it was being squeezed. That bloody lunatic would be the death of him. Unless… He wiped his sweaty forehead and built a wall around the thought, but it still broke through, 'Unless I'm the death of *him*,' he whispered to himself. He went inside, sipped a cool drink and started to feel a bit better.

Radio National, June 2001: 'More violence in the Middle East. Jewish settlers were fired on as they drove down a road bordering the Gaza Strip. A four-month-old baby was shot in the head and several settlers were wounded. In Gaza a twelve-year-old Palestinian boy was shot dead by Israeli soldiers. They claimed he was resisting arrest.'

Coates listened in despair. What was wrong with the world? He took out some bread but it was mouldy so he threw it in the bin. He opened a tin of baked beans and ate them out of the tin with a spoon. Then he went to the bedroom cupboard and took out the rifle. He opened a drawer and found a box of ammunition. He loaded the gun. A man could be murdered in his bed and the police wouldn't lift a finger to protect him. He had no choice. He had to be prepared for whatever that lunatic might do. He stood the gun near his bed.

The thought that he might wake to find Dark bending over him with a knife seemed less and less exaggerated. He began to have nightmares. One night he dreamed that he woke to find himself transformed into a deer. Dark had appeared with a knife and had cut the deer's throat. The blood that gushed from the wound was dark and ropy. Coates had woken in terror and from then on he rarely slept before light began to filter into the bedroom through the venetian blinds. He would sleep then from around five a.m. until eight a.m. Then he would get up, shattered from his terrible night, hating Dark more each day and try to eat breakfast.

After a few days, he found that he had little appetite so he would drink a cup of tea and turn the radio on.

Radio National, June 2001: 'Hopes of peace in the Middle East have been dashed again. A bomb has exploded in a street in Jerusalem. The bomb was loaded on to a donkey cart. The donkey was killed in the explosion…'

Coates suddenly put his face in his hands and started to sob. He pictured the donkey. Tears ran from between his fingers. The innocent donkey. Not comprehending its pain or its death. A dumb beast. But who was the beast? That bastard Dark was the beast, he told himself furiously. His thoughts were scrambled from lack of sleep but one thing was clear. It was Dark or him. Coates knew he was losing his grip on reality. Sitting at the kitchen table with a mug of cold tea, he said the words out loud, 'I'm losing my grip on reality.'

Radio National, June 2001: 'In Jerusalem today, the funeral of a teenage girl, a Jewish settler killed by sniper fire as she walked near a field was held. Sixteen-year-old Hepzibah Stern was shot through the heart. Ariel Sharon insists he is prepared to negotiate with Yasser Arafat but only if Palestinian violence ends.'

Coates took the rifle in his hands. To take arms against a sea of troubles. To sleep, perchance to dream. But Coates knew he would dream about Dark. There was no escape into sleep for him; there was only taking up arms. He remembered being at Tobruk. Pulling the pin of the hand grenade and tossing it. Running towards the foxhole, bayoneting left and right and the surprised faces of dying German soldiers.

He went to the cupboard where he kept his medals and took out his Victoria Cross. He pinned it on. War was cleaner in those days somehow. At least you knew where the battlefield was. He hadn't slept at all the night before and his head buzzed but he made himself a cup of tea and some toast. He found he was able to eat it. He was calm now. As calm as he had been when he charged the foxhole. He knew what he had to do. He was no dumb beast.

Carrying the rifle, Coates went outside and opened the front gate. Some strange intuition had brought Dark out into his front yard and now he stepped out on to the pavement. He smiled his blank smile.

'Are you going to shoot rats?' Dark said and Coates knew then that Dark wanted to die. Perhaps he had wanted to die for a long time. Ever since they locked him up for a crime he hadn't committed. Ever since he had been beaten almost to death. Dark smiled and made no attempt to leave.

Some people came out into their yards and someone yelled, 'Call the police!'

Coates raised the rifle and shot Dark in the left eye. Coates was a crack shot, always had been, since he was a boy on the farm shooting rabbits. His duty done, he went back into the house to wait. Dark died on the footpath, blood spreading around his head like a halo.

The Palestinian man kissed his five children goodbye that morning. His youngest daughter wasn't satisfied with a kiss and demanded a hug. He swept her up into his arms and hugged her. Then he drove his old truck down the road to where he would pick up a load of used tyres. Standing at the back of the truck he made an easy target for the Jewish settler. He shot the Palestinian in the head as he straightened to put some tyres on the truck and he fell to the ground. Blood spread around his head on the ground like some deadly bloom. The earth drank his blood and he died.

Radio National, June 2001: 'In the Middle East, Ariel Sharon has denounced Palestinian terrorism. Yasser Arafat is not doing enough to control terrorism according to Mr Sharon. The intifada must end, he said, if there is ever to be peace.'

The policeman crept up the hall, gun in hand. Coates sat at the kitchen table and the rifle leaned against the wall near the stove. The policeman's eyes flicked around the room and came to rest on the Victoria Cross.

'G'day, Digger,' he said. 'Do you want to talk about it?'

'I tried to talk about it. You wouldn't listen,' Coates said, quite calmly. He got up from the table and the policeman handcuffed him.

'I had to do it,' Coates said. 'He invaded my land. I fought to end injustice but no one would fight for me.'

They put him in a police car with flashing lights. They drove him away. Distressed faces passing the window of the car. People in their dressing gowns. Coates looked out at the unfolding day. When they stopped at the lights, he heard a magpie's joyous song. Strangely, he realised, it was going to be a beautiful day.

Fish

Memories are strange things. Slippery, like fish escaping a net, and they deceive us if they can. Make us long for things that never were – or never were the way we remember them.

It was a childhood memory of my father's that led us to the waterhole that day. He remembered it from his boyhood as a wonderful place to swim. At first he couldn't find it so we drove around in circles for what seemed like hours. It was summer and the car was like a hot box. The fact that there were five little girls squashed on the back seat and two quarrelling adults on the front seat didn't make things any cooler.

'You always do this,' my mother was saying. 'Admit that you're lost. You don't know where you are, do you? You just keep turning corners.'

'Now then, Mum,' was my father's mild reply to my mother's accusations.

No matter how much she yelled, this was all he said and that only made her yell more. She always took his forbearance as a personal insult. She cared and if he cared he would yell too. Or so her thinking seemed to go. We had our swimsuits on under our clothes so we were hot and itchy and we longed for the waterhole as sailors lost at sea must long for land.

At last we found it.

'Petrie,' my father announced, 'this is the place.' He scratched his head. 'I would've sworn it was further down the road.' He looked around. Don't remember that mountain,' he mused. 'That house wasn't there either,' he pointed to the left.

As soon as the car stopped, we threw both back doors open and rushed out into the fresh air and the cool of the forest. Because forest it was. Not the dry, ragged trees that would have been called 'bush' or 'the bush'. There were huge pine trees, or so the fish of memory tell me as I haul them in, and there was a dense, cool darkness to the place that made me think of Hansel and Gretel and the witch.

'Come on, kids,' my father called. 'Get on the path.'

So we followed him in single file along timber walkways over the tops of ravines. My mother followed too, heaving sighs and telling us that this exertion was too much for her and that the ravines gave her vertigo.

'Now then, Mum,' my father mumbled.

It wasn't until many years later, until I was a woman myself in fact, that I understood why this mild reply made my mother yell 'Shut up' at my father, so loudly that her voice echoed back out of the ravines and the forest and seemed to come at us from all directions. I hardly noticed all this because patterns of light lay like lace at my feet. I felt as if I was flying.

Then we came out into a clearing. No waterhole in sight.

'Where is it?' my mother demanded sensing a victory. 'Where is it?'

'Just keep walking,' my father told her, evenly.

Then we were there. We looked down from an immense height to a muddy waterhole. It was like looking down to the centre of the Earth. I thought about jumping in and it made my feet tingle with fear and excitement. I imagined letting myself fall down, down to that water. Sink or swim.

My mother's eyes glinted with triumph. 'Are you mad?' she snapped. 'How can they swim in that?'

My father couldn't understand it. This wasn't what he remembered. My sisters all started insisting that they could swim in that. I was silent. I was a natural mystic. I worshipped everything. Now I worshipped this hole in the ground. The thought of actually swimming in it seemed sacrilegious but now I could see that down there at the bottom of the hole there were some children swimming around. It reminded me of the story of the frogs who fell in the bucket of cream and swam round and round in circles until it turned into butter.

My father looked down at the swimming children. 'Those kids must be able to swim like fish,' he said with admiration.

My mother gave him a disgusted look. 'What are we going to do now?

They want to have a swim,' she complained. 'This can't be the one you meant,' she told him. 'You're not going to tell me that you ever swam in there.'

'There used to be a rope down the side…' my father said and I realised he wasn't sure himself any more.

'Well, we'll have to go somewhere else. What a wasted trip!' my mother sighed as she turned away.

We followed her in single file. My father followed a distance behind us and when I looked back he had a sorrowful expression on his face. Paradise lost. The vanished kingdom. The waterhole he would never find again lived on in his mind – but only there.

Not far from where we'd parked, we found a little stream, running over rocks and flowing into a small river.

'This is more like it,' my mother smiled now and put the picnic rug on the ground. Tea in a thermos, sandwiches, patty cakes and some bruised bananas were spread out on the rug and a bottle of lemonade which proved to be both warm and flat was poured. 'Yes, this is lovely,' my mother said. She was quite cheerful now.

My father threw himself down on the rug and stared up into the sky. I knew he was thinking about the waterhole that he remembered from when he was a boy. His face made me so sad I couldn't really enjoy splashing in the clean, cool water that ran over the rocks.

'It's safe here,' Mum purred lying back with her head on Dad's arm. 'Don't go near that river, though. We don't know how deep it is.'

We splashed and played happily and it was some time before we realised that one of us was missing. My sister Tania (the only redhead in the family) was nowhere to be seen. We raised the alarm and my father reared up like a startled horse and galloped off down the stream, shoes and all.

My mother kept saying, 'Oh God, oh God. Oh.' She splashed off after my father and we all followed her.

No one could find Tania and we all called her name. Then I looked down from the bank where long grass grew all the way out into the river and I could see my sister's face looking up at me from under the water while her long, red hair floated around her head. Her eyes were wide open and I screamed and felt as if my soul was flying out of my body. Blackness enveloped me. When I came to, my father was holding my sister's head while she vomited water.

'The grass,' she coughed and tried to cry but had no breath to do it. 'I thought it was the ground but the grass was growing in the water.'

She cried and vomited for some time while my ashen-faced parents asked her questions she was in no state to answer and one of my sisters poured warm lemonade down my throat because my mother said I was in shock and needed sugar.

And now it is so many years later and tomorrow is my father's funeral. We're middle-aged women now and my vigorous mother is slightly less vigorous, though passion will only die in her when she herself is dead.

She wanders from room to room as if she's looking for my father. 'I can't believe he's gone and left me,' she says, accusingly.

The heart that beat only for her, beats no more.

We are sitting in my mother's kitchen, drinking coffee and tea and eating home made muffins. One of us is missing. Tania. Kay is a physiotherapist, Lynette is a florist who runs her own shop. Brenda is a nurse. I used to be a teacher but now I only teach in a community centre two days a week. We are all married with teenage children. All except Tania. 'My vale of tears,' that's what our mother calls her. She always seems to be with men who beat her and desert her. She's also a junkie. For years, my mother and father waited for the phone call telling them that Tania had died of an overdose. It never came. It still hasn't and now it's my father who's dead…

'If she turns up off her face, I'll kill her,' Brenda vows, steaming mug of coffee held up near her own face.

Outside, the cold makes the windows of the warm kitchen steam up. The darkness is gathering and still no Tania.

My mother gets that familiar, stricken look on her face. She keeps glancing at the phone. We all know what she's thinking.

Around six when we've put a video on and opened a bottle of wine I notice that it's started to rain. Then I glance up and see Tania's face at the window. The cold, wet wind makes her red hair fly out around her head. Her wide-open eyes stare at me through the glass and I go cold. The years fall away and a scream rises in my throat. I swallow it down with the wine. Tania has been drowning all her life. I realise this for the first time.

At the window, she smiles her child's smile, mouths, 'Open the door.'

My mother looks over, sees Tania and shakes her head. 'Like a fish out of water,' she says to no one in particular.

There's a silence while we all think our own thoughts, then my mother sighs and pulls herself up out of Dad's armchair. 'Always turns up. Like a bad penny,' my mother laughs.

I laugh too but the laughter catches in my throat.

Tania slinks in from the dark like a cat. Pushing her wild, red hair back with a skinny hand she shivers. 'I always thought I'd die before Dad,' she says in a trembly voice, taking the glass of wine from my mother's hand.

It's what we've all been thinking. A shocked silence descends.

Tania laughs, uncertainly, and looks around the room from face to face. She has an addict's rough raw laugh.

'Come and sit near the fire,' my mother says, taking Tania's hands and rubbing them. 'Your hands are so cold. You look half-drowned.'

'Well, I never did learn to swim, did I?' Tania laughs and sips the wine.

'No, you didn't,' my mother says, softly.

And we sit and drink our wine while the rain flies in gusts against the roof and water runs down the windows.

Every Deed a Shining Star

It was cool and light in the church. The light was muted but reflected perfection everywhere it touched. The white marble altar and the white marble floor, the gold door of the tabernacle, the crisp, spotless white linen of the altar cloth, the rich, satiny colours of the tabernacle's covering, the pastel blue and white of the statue of Our Lady, the rich gold and red of the statue of Jesus revealing his Sacred Heart while his sad, gentle eyes seemed to look into the soul. It was a perfect world – one without stain or sin.

Every Friday, Mrs Geller and Mrs Bromley came to do the flowers on the altar. Once in the door, the noise and the confusion of the outside world fell away. Everything they did made sense and time seemed to pass more slowly than it did beyond the big, wooden doors of the church.

Mrs Geller was a lady of forty-five. She had salt and pepper hair which had once been black and a thin, stern face. Her body, though, was soft and rounded and she wore colourful skirts and comfortable tops in summer and tracksuits (but only the best quality) in winter. She would have described herself as a natural leader, though others might have put it differently.

Some of the other ladies who took care of the church found her a bit bossy. 'But she's a good soul,' they'd say. 'She means well.'

Mrs Bromley was Mrs Geller's opposite in every way. Thin and fragile-looking with hair of a colour somewhere between grey and mouse and a personality to match. Mrs Geller thought Mrs Bromley was slightly younger than she was; though she would sooner have cut out her tongue than tell her so.

Mrs Geller's booming voice would echo through the church, issuing orders to Mrs Bromley, while Mrs Bromley hurried to carry them out.

'Put the roses over there, near the Sacred Heart. The red goes well there. Are the lilies in water yet? You know how quickly they dry out. Now where's that vase, the one with the fluted top? You know the one I mean.'

Even if she didn't, Mrs Bromley would never dare admit it. She was on the run the whole time she was in the church with Mrs Geller but if Mrs Geller moved it was only to supervise what Mrs Bromley was doing. Sometimes she stood near the altar as if she was a priest presiding over some ritual.

These two were not on first name terms, though they had been doing the flowers together for years now. One thing they did have in common – both were childless. Mrs Bromley appeared to accept this with the same stoic calm with which she accepted everything else but Mrs Geller had let this disappointment affect her. Mrs Bromley had always thought that this was what made Mrs Geller so abrupt and critical of others.

Mrs Bromley always tried to see the other side of the story – it was her nature to be compassionate. Mrs Geller, on the other hand, had firm views on everything, especially sexual matters. Having no children of her own gave her time to catch every bit of gossip circulating in the parish and to meddle in matters she should have stayed out of.

'My mother used to say,' she would tell Mrs Bromley, 'that we should make every deed a shining star, but dearie me, there's people in this parish, people who sit in this church every Sunday who don't do that! Not at all! I suppose you know about Mr Finney and Miss Black. Shameless how some people carry on, and sitting there every Sunday as if butter wouldn't melt, I ask you.'

In fact, she rarely asked anyone anything. She was much too busy telling and criticising and judging and Mrs Bromley was the perfect listener. The passive, accepting ear into which Mrs Geller could pour her rigid opinions and her scandalous stories.

Having been childless all her married life, Mrs Geller could also pour scorn on those weaklings who resorted to contraception. She was even more scathing about those who succumbed to the temptations of the flesh to the extent that they forgot their marriage vows. Never having been pretty, she watched with delight as the years destroyed the beauty of others. She would almost dance with amusement at the foolishness of those who 'tarted themselves up' by colouring their hair or wearing make-up.

'Old Mrs Larkin. What a hoot! Did you see what she had on last Sunday? It was all I could do not to laugh in her face. And her hair dyed that colour! Lord, she must be sixty if she's a day.'

Mrs Bromley would nod or say 'Mmmn' during these outbursts while she carefully placed flowers just so. Her flower arrangements were always perfect and harmonious, as her life seemed to be. Her husband was a quiet, shy man who had worked in the same office – a printery – since the day he had left school in 1969. They always went to Hervey Bay for their holidays because they owned a little beach house there. It was a small, modest place appropriate to small, modest lives such as theirs. Children would have been almost too demanding and too dramatic, Mrs Bromley thought. God really knew best, sometimes.

Mrs Geller's husband Len was a builder and, even though he'd declared himself bankrupt several times, he had still managed to amass a considerable fortune, which he guarded with great tenacity from the grandiose schemes and outright greed of Mrs Geller. She lacked for nothing and told anyone who would listen about the national disgrace of people being paid to do nothing. Namely those too under-skilled, undereducated or too unfortunate to find a job.

She decried instances of 'waste' of public money which she read about in the paper or saw on current affairs programs on television. She angrily bemoaned the wrongness of people being paid to do nothing while her husband paid her to sit in her luxurious house and do nothing much at all. She had a gardener and a cleaning lady and time on her hands and for her a little knowledge was indeed a dangerous thing.

Mrs Geller never really paid much attention to Mrs Bromley. She was simply there, a beige, muted backdrop who existed in Mrs Geller's mind purely to highlight her colourful clothes, to do her bidding and to receive her verbal poison drop by drop. Mrs Bromley always seemed imperturbable. Reliable, that was the word. Like an old piece of furniture.

Even Mrs Geller noticed, though, when Mrs Bromley began arriving at the church late on Fridays, pale and twitchy and with red-rimmed eyes. She had also blonded her hair and had started wearing make-up. She no longer wore those respectable skirts and sensible blouses but had bought herself some dresses. Pretty ones too. No good could come of such things, Mrs Geller told herself.

Then, one Friday, Mrs Geller began once more on the topic of the appalling Finney-Black affair. 'A married man with three children and his wife is such a nice little thing. That Miss Black – Black by name and Black by nature if you ask me.' On and on she went in a similar vein.

So caught up was she in her sermon that she didn't notice at first that Mrs Bromley was near collapse. She had to sit on the big wooden chair that the priest sometimes used during Mass, to recover. Mrs Geller had never seen Mrs Bromley so upset. In fact, she had never seen her upset at all and yet she was clearly on the brink of tears. Mrs Geller grew very still and fixed her eyes on Mrs Bromley because she knew all the signs. Mrs Bromley was going to crack. She was going to confess. Born and bred a Catholic, the urge to confess was second nature to her and would not be denied.

'I don't know what I'm going to do,' said Mrs Bromley who was now a terrible pasty colour under her gleaming, blonded hair. 'I never meant it to go this far.' Tears brimmed in her eyes and she blinked them away. Her voice echoed off the marble floor, off the whiter than white walls of the church. Jesus' sad eyes watched her as Mrs Bromley confessed to an affair.

Oh, what a sinner she was! She then broke down completely and what she said was incomprehensible. Mrs Geller's pulse was racing. The words 'affair' and 'sinner' had flown to her heart like arrows. A passionate glow of self-righteousness formed around her salt and pepper head like a halo. How wonderful to be as she was! This pathetic woman spilling her sordid secrets in God's house, in front of the Sacred Heart, could never be her. All of that business had been safely put away under lock and key. The thought of Mrs Bromley with this man, whoever he was, was disgusting, indecent.

Mrs Geller had not said one word and Mrs Bromley found a tissue and dried her eyes. There was fear in her eyes; she realised her mistake. A priest might give absolution but Mrs Geller would not. The atmosphere was now so strained that Mrs Bromley soon pleaded a headache and went home.

Standing at the altar rails, Mrs Geller threw a look of contempt after her, then sighed. She would have to do all the flowers herself now. The statue of the Virgin turned her mild blue eyes on Mrs Geller and looked at her lovingly. Mrs Geller sighed again and mopped up the water Mrs Bromley had spilled as she carried vases in her shaking hands.

'It's a wonder she didn't smash something,' she muttered to herself. Then the thought came to her that perhaps she had.

Mrs Bromley no longer came to arrange flowers in the church on Fridays. Her place was taken by Mrs Beggs and what a trial that was for Mrs Geller. Mrs Beggs talked incessantly. She was terribly opinionated and could never be budged from any position she took, no matter how much Mrs Geller argued. No matter how she tried to enlighten her.

Mrs Beggs's husband was a union leader and Mrs Beggs said the bosses were too greedy. 'That's what causes all the trouble.'

Mrs Geller's jaw dropped and she tried to gasp something out but Mrs Beggs smoothly steamrollered her to one side with a verbal barrage that left her in its wake, like a truck leaving a rush of air as it passed. No matter how much Mrs Geller tried to reason with her, she just put her head down and went on talking, something like a horse pulling a heavy load. Mrs Geller had gone to Father Brady and had Mrs Bromley removed from her church duties. She wasn't fit to set foot in the church – anyone could see that.

Then one Friday in late spring, Mrs Beggs hurried into the church with a bucket of flowers – snapdragons, mayflowers and roses – and whispered breathlessly, 'Did you hear? Mrs Bromley's run off with some man. They say she's pregnant.'

Mrs Geller dropped the vase she was holding and scintillating shards of glass went everywhere. The light bounced off each and every fragment on the white marble floor; even the tiniest pieces threw brilliant light and Mrs Geller stared, amazed that so much beauty could come out of a smashed vase.

'I'll get the dustpan,' said Mrs Beggs, but then she went on in her unstoppable way, 'Not only that but poor David Bromley's tried to kill himself. He's in the psych ward at the hospital. Isn't it terrible?'

This last was said with the tone of malicious joy that would be found in a child's voice as they announced that the school had burned down but Mrs Geller knew better than to try to stem the flow. It couldn't be done. Mrs Beggs chattered on but Mrs Geller had stopped listening. She was staring at the incandescent gleam of the shattered glass. Every deed a shining star, she was thinking.

When Mrs Geller got home, she saw an envelope propped up near the phone with her name written on it (Muriel, in green ink). It was Len's handwriting. She walked to it as if she was sleepwalking (she had been for years, as she was about to find out) and as she picked it up and started to open it she suddenly knew the contents as surely as if she had already read them. In fact she had an inexplicable feeling of déjà vu.

There had been others, Len wrote, but he and Yvonne were in love. Yvonne? That was Mrs Bromley's name. What a coincidence. Then a hand seemed to twist her heart and squeeze it. Yvonne was Mrs Bromley and Len had left her for that mouse.

'We're leaving town to start a new life…'

Here Mrs Geller started to laugh and she laughed until tears ran down her face. 'A new life!' she screamed with laughter. She had to sit down.

'You can keep the house and the car and half of the investments. I've already changed them into your name…'

It had all been planned; like a military coup.

'If you curb your spending, you can live very comfortably on the interest.'

She threw the letter on the floor and turned away from it with a cold, shocked feeling that wasn't anger and yet must be anger.

She sat on the velvet armchair near a sunlit window and decided that tomorrow she would have the gardener dig out all the roses. She didn't like roses; they were Len's and she had no further use for them. Tomorrow she would go to Mass and pray for Len and Mrs Bromley. If those hypocrites in the congregation thought that Muriel Geller would run and hide, they were wrong! She had nothing to be ashamed of. This business would never be her downfall. She would forgive until the whole town was struck dumb with wonder.

Len had now retired from the field and the true story would be the one she told. Len didn't like babies, as Mrs Bromley would discover. Looking out the window and contemplating the roses she would shortly destroy, she almost felt sorry for her. She remembered the abortion Len had forced on her when she was young and foolish, in the first year of their marriage. The abortion that had left her infertile. It was Mrs Bromley she felt sorry for. How strange.

She slipped her shoes off and went to feed Miso, the cat. The cat rubbed up against her legs, purring. She ran herself a bath and poured in lots of bubble bath. She was looking forward to what she now realised was her first peaceful night in their queen-sized bed.

The Sewing Circle

The terrible stories are always true; the pretty stories most people learn to take with a grain of salt. The ladies of the sewing circle told both kinds but it was the terrible, shivery ones that they remembered. Often they secretly cursed the teller. Who would want such things in their minds? In their memories? Yet the teller had sometimes carried their story for twenty years or more, finally laying it down in the intimacy of the sewing circle as a weary traveller drops the luggage they have carried with them halfway around the world.

Eleni was making a christening robe. Sherry was embroidering a tapestry of swans on a lake with a cottage in the background, Christine was working on a baby's quilt. Lisa was making a tutu for her ballerina daughter – it was so white it made her eyes ache and she wore surgeon's gloves to sew it.

Christine had started the sewing circle five years before and offered her house as a meeting place. Sometimes Christine made wall hangings. A woman friend sold them for her in a craft shop. They sold well. They were full of chaos and turmoil. It was hard to believe that quiet, shy Christine had made them.

'Unfortunately people see their own lives in them,' Christine said sadly. 'That's what I think.'

But Lisa said, 'No. Their own lives are boring. They're interested in passion and pain but only if they can hang it on the wall.'

Lisa was the thinker of the group. In her other life as an academic she had made a lot of enemies because she was a terror for the truth. 'There was more blood and guts in that university some days than you'd find in the average butcher's shop,' she had once said. 'That's what I'd hear as I walked up to those impressive colonnaded walkways, the metallic sound of steel on steel. Knives being sharpened.'

What the other members of the group heard was the click, click, click of Lisa's brain. She had an intelligence that almost terrified them.

'I used to work in a television station, you know,' Lisa said. 'Just the local television station in a provincial town, a very provincial town. A girl my own age came to work there. We were both twenty-four. I had just finished my undergraduate degree in arts, which qualified me to be a typist in that town. I just looked on it as filling in time before I went on to postgraduate studies – which never happened until much later because I got pregnant and got married, but that's another story. This girl was blonde, really pretty, intense and ambitious but she had these strange, dead eyes. Ice blue, fish eyes they were – cold, really cold. I never liked her. She was married but she was a real career woman – no children, thank you very much. It was 1975. Kids had become pretty unfashionable. Women wanted to work, to travel, to "find themselves".'

The women nodded and sewed on, eyes down.

'Well, anyway, sometime that year, Fish Eyes – her name was Marion – got pregnant but told no one. I mean no one.'

'Not her husband?' Eleni looked up from the lace she was pinning on to the robe. 'Not even him?'

'Especially not him! He wanted children. She'd told everyone that. She didn't want to be pregnant. She'd just been plucked from the typing pool and made weather girl. She was on the way up so the pregnancy was a catastrophe. Her husband was an engineer and he was getting good money. She boasted about it constantly as such bimbos will. She was getting next to nothing for being a weather girl. She couldn't afford an abortion unless her husband paid and she knew he never would. A backyard abortion was something she would never risk. She began to fill out but it suited her. She'd been unnaturally thin. The pregnancy hardly showed. Time went by. No baby. Then about a year after she'd been made weather girl, she had a nervous breakdown. Cracked up and was carted off to the psych ward at the local hospital and then to a mental home. She stayed there for two years. What about the baby, I hear you cry.'

'Never said a word.' Sherry was leaning so far forward she looked as if she might fall off her seat.

'Oh well, I won't tell you what happened, then,' Lisa teased.

Cries of outrage filled the room.

'Okay, okay. Settle down. You're turning into a rabble.'

Needles started moving again.

'Marion comes out of the mental home, so changed that people who'd known her all her life passed her in the street without a flicker of recognition. She was a broken woman. By then her husband had left her. Soon, though, she enrols at a teacher's training college and becomes a teacher.'

'A teacher?' Christine looked disbelieving.

Lisa nodded.

'Is it true?' Christine demanded earnestly.

Lisa laughed. 'Would I lie to you?'

'She must have changed a lot.' Eleni was staring off into the distance.

'There was method in her madness, as you will see.' Lisa looked wise and all-knowing, which was slightly unnerving.

'Wine?' Christine produced a chilled, green bottle.

The wine was poured and eight eager eyes focused on Lisa.

'Where was I? Ah yes. She became a teacher but once she had her diploma there was only one school she wanted to teach at. A school called Westville State School – so called because it was on the west side of town, not far in fact from where Marion and her husband used to live. Marion worked as a supply teacher for three years until Westville State School took her on.'

Lisa sipped her wine. Sewing had been put to one side. No one moved.

Eleni was staring at Lisa and finally she burst out, 'Why Lisa? Why?'

'I'm coming to it. Patience. There was a garden that ran the full length of the space between two school buildings. Marion took care of it and then the whole school garden. She expanded the gardens so that they were in bloom all year round. It usually won a prize at the annual garden festival in the town. Well, years went by. Fifteen years to be exact. Marion died of cancer of the uterus.'

'What?' Eleni spilt some of her wine. 'She's dead?'

'Yes. Comes to all of us, Eleni,.' Lisa gave a devilish grin.

More wine was poured.

'After Marion died, building work started at the Westville school. A new building was going up. The garden between the two buildings was dug out. Guess what they found?'

Christine gulped her wine. 'Not the baby?' she said in dread.

'The skeleton. The baby's skeleton. She'd had the baby, probably smothered it. I could be kind and say it was born dead but remembering those fish eyes I'm sure she killed it. Then she drove to the school, in the middle of the night I suppose, since it was the only time no one would have seen her. Hidden from view between the buildings, she dug a deep hole and buried the baby in the garden. All the time she was at the school she was near its grave and the flowers she grew were, in effect, flowers she was putting on its grave.'

Not a sound from the sewing circle.

'She had to be near the garden because of her guilt. She had to tend the garden so that no one else could find the remains. She became a primary school teacher so that she could make amends by performing some service for the children she hadn't killed.'

'How do you know all this?' asked Sherry.

'It was in the paper about the skeleton being found and I heard about her working at the school from people who'd worked with both of us at the television station. We'd always believed she was pregnant. When I read about the skeleton being found, I knew what had happened.'

Cars could be heard in the street outside. Far away a siren screamed. Birds chirruped in Carol's garden. A clock ticked somewhere in the house.

At last Eleni said, 'Poor lady.'

Christine turned on Lisa furiously. 'You're a cold one, Lisa. I sometimes think you have no feelings at all.' She was nearly crying. Then she took up the baby's quilt she was working on, looked at it as if realising for the first time what it was, hesitated, then started to sew again.

This was when everyone realised that Christine had tried for years to have a baby but had repeatedly miscarried. Lisa wore a defiant look. The story was true and the truth must be told and it must be faced. That was the rule Lisa lived by.

'When Costas and I first arrived in Australia, I hated it.' Eleni spoke softly, smoothing out some lace and pinning it in place. 'There was this man. He interviewed us and checked our passports when we were leaving the migrant hostel to move into our own place. He was sitting behind a desk in a room with pale green walls. Even now when I remember those walls, I feel sick. We got here in 1967.'

She set her needle in place and with the precision of a surgeon stitching a wound began to attach the lace to the christening robe. 'I thought Australians were savages. It was because of this horrible man. He had short hair, all greased and combed into place. Set like concrete. He was some kind of public servant. Black trousers, white shirt and red and white striped tie. Not young, not old.' Eleni laughed. 'The funny part was he looked almost Greek. Like a wog, you know,' she added with a grin.

The sewing circle flinched a bit at the word. It was one of those words they were a bit ashamed of; they never used those words themselves.

'Costas was taken into another room and this man started asking me about where I came from, how long had we been married, did we have children – that kind of thing. I was very pretty then. Thin, not like now,' she laughed indicating her bulky body, 'and very innocent – it was expected.' She frowned.

Quick, skilful fingers worked away as she went on. 'I answered him as best I could. My understanding of English was not that good. I told him that Costas and I both came from Crete and that we hadn't been married long, no children as yet.'

'Was he filling in a form?'

'He was playing a game.'

'What game?'

'I don't think it has a name or if it does, I don't know it.' Sparks shot out of Eleni's black eyes.

'I suppose you didn't have the words to tell him off,' Lisa said.

'He was looking at me in such a strange way. He asked me if my husband was big and Costas is not tall so I said he wasn't. He smirked. Then he asked me if he gave me what I wanted in bed. Well! I was shocked! On Crete only a prostitute would be spoken to in such a way.

I was horrified and he smiled. An evil smile – I don't know how else to describe it. I was confused. He looked straight at me. "You know," he said, "they do operations to restore virginity in Greek girls. Is that what you did? Fooled your husband?"' Eleni laughed sadly and put the robe down.

The group looked up, waiting.

'At last I understood. He was trying to degrade me as a woman and as a Greek. I felt like crying but I wouldn't cry in front of him in that room with those horrible green walls. I just stared at him and pretended to be as stupid as he thought I was.'

'What did he do then?' asked Lisa.

'Picked up a pen and started pushing it backwards and forwards between his fingers, giving me this smirk all the time.'

'What was he trying to prove?' Christine wondered.

'With the pen? I understood it to mean that he wanted to have sex with me,' Eleni grinned.

The sewing circle exploded with laughter.

'That's pathetic,' Sherry said, still laughing. 'Bloody pathetic.'

'He was…how do you put it? Not my type.' Eleni began to sew again.

'He was a bigoted clown,' Lisa said.

This made them laugh again but with a new note of edginess. Lisa had gone to the heart of the matter as she always did.

'What happened then?' Christine asked.

'He picked up this big heavy stamp and stamped my form three or four times. I felt as if he was stamping me, crushing me. My head started to ache. When I'm angry I get tired, so when we walked down the corridor and out into the sunshine, I felt as if I could hardly move. I had to put my head on Costas's shoulder in the taxi on the way to our new flat I was so sleepy. The first thing I did in our new flat was get in the shower and wash and wash and wash myself. My skin was so red I looked like a lobster!'

Eleni laughed but now the others didn't laugh. They were too sad for Eleni and for themselves. They were thinking about barriers, lines on maps and mental prisons but Lisa was thinking that man was probably dead now and good riddance.

'Costas knew there was something wrong but I wouldn't tell him. I still haven't.'

Slowly they all began stitching again.

'This christening robe is for my new granddaughter. Imagine my granddaughter being called Frances Rebecca Smith! When I was a girl on Crete, I could never have imagined a granddaughter called Frances Rebecca Smith.' Eleni smoothed the christening robe with her long, brown hands.

'My son Martin was always secretive,' Sherry began. 'Always. Even when he was a baby he had a secretive smile.'

They all nodded.

'Gavin says I imagined it but I didn't. He was like a little spy with a head full of secrets, a beautiful little spy. Hair as black as coal – born with it and it only got darker as he grew. His eyes were blue to begin with but they went green when he was four. He never let anyone close. Refused the breast, so he had to have the bottle.

'When he was three, he disappeared one day and I found him eating poppy seeds in the garden. He slept all the rest of the day and all night too. He woke up at three in the morning, pale and angry. That was the first time he disappeared and after that I think all he ever wanted was to find a way to disappear for good. I loved him more than the other two. Spoiled him, I suppose. It was as if I knew what was going to happen. He was so bright, like a little man when he looked at you, as if he'd been here before. Not that I believe in reincarnation, but how can you know?

'When he was nine, he asked me to buy a magician's box of tricks that he'd seen in a toyshop. I bought it for him and from then on he spent every minute practising card tricks, making eggs disappear. Gavin thought it was funny but I didn't. It was obsessive. He'd get so angry if you interrupted one of his tricks. He'd yell and throw things. I'd smack him and he'd look at me as if I was mad. One day he said, "I'll make myself disappear. I will!" I went cold all over. After that, I left him alone.

'By the time he was ten, he was being hired for kid's birthday parties as a magician. He had to have a suit, white shirts, a tie to perform in. When I saw him perform, it was like watching a professional. He was so smooth, so polished, so funny. The way he would pretend to muck up a trick and then turn it into an even better one. Making the kids laugh – and the adults! They laughed more than the kids did.

'By thirteen he was a regular on a kid's show on television. He had something I can't quite describe. Some kind of gift. Born with it like that jet-black hair. He was always polite to me by this time but he always went his own way. It was as if he had a plan and everything and everyone was just a stepping stone to something better.

'Then two days before his fourteenth birthday he went out the front door wearing his school uniform and disappeared. Just like that. As if he'd decided to carry out his threat at long last. Some woman said she saw him down near the bus terminal. Other people saw him other places. The police did their best but he was gone. Just gone. I told you all that I'd lost one of my sons. That's what I tell people. That's what the police told me. That he was dead. It's simpler to believe that – I'd suffer less if I could – but I don't believe it. In fact, in my heart I know that he did what he said he'd do – he made himself disappear.

'Two weeks after he vanished, a statement from the bank came addressed to him. The account he'd opened in his own name once he turned twelve. There was only five dollars left in it. The rest had been withdrawn. In Melbourne. Since then, I've always believed that he was in Melbourne all the time the police were searching for him in Sydney.'

'Did you tell the police?' Christine asked.

'I couldn't see the point. I knew he wouldn't let them find him. It's hard to explain but I never felt that he belonged to me. Not the way I felt with the others. Not even when he was a toddler. He only ever belonged to himself.'

'The more you love a child like that, the more they slip away. Is that it?' Lisa asked.

Sherry nodded.

'It must've broken your heart.' Christine looked into Sherry's eyes.

'Sometimes I can make myself believe that he's dead. Then some talent show will come on television and there'll be a magician. I'll look at them, try to guess their age, try to guess how he would have changed but they're usually pretty hopeless and he was always so professional and his looks were so distinctive. I'd know if it was him. I'd know.' Sherry stared into the distance.

'Then perhaps,' Lisa was uncertain how to proceed, 'perhaps he is dead.'

'No.' Sherry cut the white embroidery cotton. 'You know what I think? I've had years to think about it – twenty years, in fact. I think the magic was just to fill in time, to make the money he needed to leave and to keep him occupied until he was ready to disappear. I think that's all he really wanted – to be free, to be on his own – and he went about it methodically and obsessively the way he did everything. That's what I think.'

'You don't have to answer this but if he was reincarnated who do you think he was?' asked Lisa.

Christine threw Lisa an angry look.

Sherry saw it. 'It's okay, Christine. It doesn't upset me to talk about it. That's all I have left of him – memories and conversation. That's all any of us have in the end. You'll probably laugh, Lisa, but I think he was a sorcerer.'

'King Arthur's Merlin?' Lisa always had to know.

'He was like no one else. So strange and beautiful. I'll always be glad I knew him even for those few years.' Sherry was searching for a certain shade of blue cotton. 'Maybe one day I'll open the door and he'll be standing there but…'

'You don't believe it,' Eleni said.

'No, I don't.' Sherry found the cotton, threaded her needle and started placing neat, blue stitches on to the tapestry sky.

Christine sighed, 'I was going to tell you about my little dog but you've all told such wonderful stories today. My little story seems so…little,' she smiled shyly.

'We love little stories, don't we, girls?' Lisa was being supportive.

'Love 'em,' Sherry said. 'Big ones, little ones – we love 'em all.'

Encouraged but not quite sure they weren't mocking her, Christine placed a stitch in ribbon the colour of clotted cream that bordered her quilt and began. 'When I was twelve, I got a little dog named Fudge for my birthday. Twelve is such a wonderful age because everything still seems possible. Self-consciousness is beginning but hasn't quite begun so there's a curious double life where you can be a child and yet know, as you never have before, that you are one. Fudge was the exact colour of the caramel fudge I always bought at the school fete. She was a chihuahua crossed with something – we never knew what. She'd been dumped and my father bought her from the pound.'

Lisa soon lost interest and started to measure one of the layers of the tutu. She drifted off into another story altogether. Carey. Why did she think of him? Probably because he had black hair and green eyes and was a magician in his own sweet way. He'd made her understand why orgasm was called the little death. Hawaii. Palm trees had never looked the same since Carey.

'Fudge had black lines around her eyes, almost as if she was wearing kohl eyeliner and everything matched. She was caramel, black and cream. Even her claws were black...'

Fingernails raking his back. No, no, not here! Not here, no not... Caramel tan. Ice cream. Madness. They ate almost nothing. Drank margaritas instead. When room service brought food, they had food fights and then licked it off each other's skin.

'She barked at lights and whistles. Hated flutes and she would stand on her back legs and walk when she felt threatened. Sometimes she bit my friends but her teeth were so little...'

Biting, biting, but it felt so good. The images went through her mind like scenes from a film.

Then far away she heard Christine's voice saying, 'There was nothing that could be done and the vet said the kindest thing was to put her down. So we buried her in the backyard and my father planted a jacaranda seedling. It was about a foot high when he planted it. I passed our old house recently. You should see that tree today, towering up into the sky. Poor little Fudge. I couldn't help but remember her.'

When she woke the next morning, he was gone. No note. Nothing. She buried her face in the pillow that still smelled of him and cried until she was sick. Holiday romance. For him. For her, though, it was love or addiction or maybe both. She didn't know his address or his phone number and she suspected that he was married. He was gone. He made himself disappear.

Christine was picking up wine glasses and straightening cushions when Eric walked in, home from lawn bowls.

'Another sewing bee bites the dust,' he laughed. 'What on earth do you find to talk about?'

Christine raised her eyebrows. 'You wouldn't be interested,' she told him.

'It's just girl talk. You know, nothing too serious.'

When he looked at her, she was smiling but not at him. She was smiling to herself, like a sphinx.

Objectivity

He hated it when they used a monkey. The rats and mice didn't bother him so much, even though they were more cartoon cute. The monkeys, though, looked like little old men with their wise, wrinkled faces. He hated the fact that they had hands and expressive faces and the way someone would have to hold their wrists as if they were fractious children.

It was the rhesus monkey they used the day his nightmare began.

Only that morning, Professor Kubik had been lecturing him about scientific objectivity. 'Without that, we're no use to anyone. We're scientists and we have to prove everything. That's our job.'

So the rhesus monkey was brought in that day; just before midday it was. A funny little old man creature and someone held its wrists. It screamed and struggled.

They had to find the correct dosage for a drug, so the monkey was injected with it. Then the thing he could never forget happened. The monkey screwed up its face, like a child that had been hurt. Its face went purple and it died. Just like that. Its body was put to one side on a trolley. The procedure was repeated and this time the monkey didn't die and it was put back in its cage. But Brown didn't look at that monkey. He looked at the dead one; at its little body discarded on a trolley. He kept seeing its face contorted in pain…

'Are you okay? You look a bit odd, Brown,' Professor Kubik remarked. His face sneered though his voice was soft and reasonable.

'I'm fine,' Brown told him. 'Fine.' But his heart was racing and he wasn't fine at all.

The change in Kubik was hardly noticeable at first. In fact, Brown was the only one who noticed it. The others seemed to see nothing and Brown began to fear for his sanity.

'Do you believe in ghosts?' he asked Tippler one day.

Tippler was a fellow scientist but he was also an uncomplicated, red-headed comedian who seemed to think that life was a huge joke and he was able to find humour in almost anything. Brown had already faced the fact that Tippler was destined for those heady scientific heights that he himself would never achieve. Sunshine for Tippler; shadow for Brown.

Tippler rolled his eyes and wailed, 'Ghosts. Ghoooosts!'

Brown felt his face burning with humiliation. 'Have you noticed anything different about Kubik,' he finally stammered out.

'Nothing except that the old bastard's had a humility bypass. Did you hear him this morning? You know what the Germans say? *Eigenlob stinkt.* It means self-praise stinks. Kubik's obviously never heard it.' Tippler threw back his head and laughed. 'He thinks he's a genius, you know.'

'His hands…'

'His hands. What about them?'

'They're different.'

Tippler's smile faded and he stepped back as if to distance himself from something that he was beginning to think wasn't funny.

'His hands are a lot hairier,' Brown blundered on.

Tippler shook his head at Brown's words and his smile was now the smile of a man not completely at ease.

'You have a look at his hands,' Brown pleaded. 'Next time you see him, take a look and tell me what you think.'

Tippler grinned and started humming the theme from *The Twilight Zone.* 'Yes, I'll do that,' he laughed, backing away.

Brown knew he would do no such thing. He would tell the others, though. He might even tell Kubik.

Something strange was going on. Kubik had told them that as scientists they had to prove everything. That was true, of course, but part of proving something scientifically was observation. Something terrible was happening to Professor Kubik and Brown could hardly believe that the others couldn't see it. The next day he noticed the professor's teeth. His incisors were now so much longer and sharper that Brown actually looked from face to face expecting some sign of dismay or curiosity but Tippler, Stevens, Grainger and Dragovitch – the whole scientific team in fact, apart from him – were hanging on Kubik's every word.

Brown wanted to shout, 'Can't you see? Look at this man! Look at him! He's turning into an ape. A rhesus monkey in fact, just like the one he killed.'

Of course he said nothing. He watched and listened as Kubik dissected a rat he had injected with cancer cells. Brown thought he saw Tippler looking thoughtfully at Kubik's hands, covered by surgeon's gloves, but when Brown tried to catch his eye, Tippler wouldn't look at him. Under the gloves, Kubik's hands, Brown knew, were covered in thick, dark fur. And under his clothes? Kubik could cover the fur with his clothes, he could shave his face and hands but Brown had noticed other things that would eventually be impossible to hide. Professor Kubik was shrinking and his eyes were changing colour.

Brown had to talk to someone, so he cornered Tippler again. He had to run to catch up to him. 'Did you see what's happened to his teeth?' he asked, catching at Tippler's arm.

Tippler turned a pitying face on him. 'Brown, you need to see a doctor. You've been working too hard and quite frankly no one here thinks you're cut out for the work we do. Have you thought about becoming a vet?'

Brown's eyes showed genuine concern and Brown was fleetingly sad that his shadow was spilling over into Tippler's sunshine. 'It's the rhesus monkey he killed,' Brown muttered, almost to himself.

'What?'

'He killed the monkey and something happened. I felt it at the time. It's as if the monkey's ghost is taking him over.'

Tippler grabbed Brown by the shoulders and gently shook him. 'Brown, listen to what you're saying. Listen to yourself. Monkeys just die. They don't have ghosts. They're animals. Beasts. I'm shocked to hear a scientist such as yourself talking such dangerous rubbish. A man cannot become a monkey.'

'You believe that a monkey can become a man. Darwin, evolution, all that – you believe that, don't you?' Brown knew that he was babbling and felt ashamed.

'Brown,' Tippler said, with infinite gentleness, 'it's all one-way traffic, as you know. We can go forward but we can never go back, evolutionally speaking. I'm trying to reason with you because we all hope you will take action to help yourself.'

'And if I don't?' he asked, wondering exactly what Tippler meant.

'Surely you can see that we can't allow you to run around saying that one of the most respected professors in this institute is turning into a monkey? If you won't get help, action will have to be taken.'

Tippler walked away shaking his head and Brown realised in that instant that he would have to walk away too. For good. He took his white coat off and threw it away in disgust. When he looked up to the gallery, he saw two of his colleagues watching him, staring at the white coat that was lying at his feet. He didn't care, not now. He walked out of the medical research building and he knew he would never go back. Outside, he walked into a world of sunshine and birdsong. It was spring and the beauty of the world hit him with an almost physical force. It was like coming back from the dead.

Two years later, he qualified as a vet and got a job at a zoo. He had decided to dedicate his life to caring for animals. On his first day at the zoo, he looked into the rhesus monkey enclosure while being shown around by another vet. He noticed that one of the monkeys sat apart from all the others. There were trees and bushes and tall grasses to play in but this monkey sat alone while all the others swung and chattered and wrestled.

'Is that monkey sick?' Brown asked Tischler, his new work colleague.

'Oh,' Tischler laughed, 'that's a strange story.'

'What do you mean?'

'Well, they found that monkey running around in a laboratory. At first they thought he must have escaped from one of the cages but they counted all the monkeys and there were none missing. I don't know why they didn't keep him for their experiments but for some reason they decided to bring him here.'

A strange feeling came over Brown as he remembered reading in the paper about Professor Kubik's disappearance. Several unnamed colleagues from the research institute hinted at suicide, claiming Kubik hadn't been himself for some time.

'The monkey's been with us for about eighteen months now,' Tischler went on. 'A funny character brought him here. A real joker. He was laughing and joking right up until he had to hand over the monkey. Then he had tears in his eyes and said something about it all being so tragic. I've got no idea what he meant.'

'What was his name? Do you remember?'

'I remember it because it was so like mine. Tippler, his name was. He was tall and skinny and he had red hair.'

'Tippler…'

'Perhaps. He seemed to have a real bond with the monkey. It held on to his coat. We had to prise its hands off. He showed us how to hold its wrists.'

Brown stared into space.

'Come on,' Tischler laughed, 'the meerkats are just around the corner. They're a big hit with the public and we're quite fond of them ourselves. When you watch them, you can't help laughing. They're the comedians of the zoo.'

Brown suddenly stopped walking. 'Listen, Tischler,' he said. 'I have to ask you a favour. Would you mind if I didn't treat the monkeys? You see, I have a kind of phobia.'

Tishler looked at Brown. He had sensed some kind of vulnerability in him from the start. 'Of course,' he told his new colleague. 'The monkeys are my favourites. I'm happy to treat them. Sometimes when you look into their eyes…'

'Please,' Brown pleaded, 'don't say any more. It upsets me. It's my phobia.'

'Of course.'

Then the two men walked on until they came to the meerkat enclosure and Brown realised with infinite regret that all his efforts to escape the past were completely useless. Each and every meerkat reminded him of Tippler.

Slipstream

Kerry thought that perhaps it was because of never quite being told the truth. The leitmotif that ran through her childhood. Perhaps it was that. The insecurity or something. She didn't really know and didn't believe that knowing would do her any good. Perhaps being shielded from the truth made the truths of human existence so hard to bear later on. Was that what made her seek dreams she would never have to wake up from?

Dreams were not what she found. What she found was marijuana, Serepax, speed and then heroin. Even following this progression, which seemed like destiny at the time, she still felt pain. And fear. More fear in the end than she had ever felt before. Her whole life seemed to be a search for a silver bullet. In the middle of the night, she knew there was no such thing but when the sun came up she resumed the search. At school socials she used to drink to get high (outside the hall, with the other renegades) because the experience of the bright lights, the shiny floor, the loud music and the smell of aftershave, perfume and desperation was so gruesome. Vomiting on the grass outside the hall was a kind of ritual. Smoking to look cool and in control led to smoking a joint. Then somewhere along the line it changed. She didn't drink to get high any more. She went out each day looking for a way to be extinguished, as if her soul was too heavy for her to carry. Consciousness became torture. Consciousness was the shakes and being sick and craving the drug and fearing not getting it.

She had children because in an absent-minded moment she thought they would make her part of something. The human race, for example. Left by the father of her first baby, she sat night after night in front of the television screen and listened to the baby cry in another room. She had so little furniture that the sound echoed. It was a lonely sound. The baby cried with a will, as if she already knew her birth hadn't been a good idea. The baby's young father, drug-addicted and unemployed, obviously thought the same thing. When he left, he stole the milk money she kept in a honey jar on top of the fridge, and she laughed and cried at the same time, standing there on the cold lino with months of winter to go through yet, holding the empty honey jar in her hand. The milk money had been her attempt at normality.

Paradise was to be found floating in her bloodstream after she'd shot up. Otherwise it was nowhere to be found. Once she dreamed she had the riddle of the universe tattooed on the palm of her hand but it was in a language she couldn't decipher. Another day like all the others dawned after this dream, even though she'd hoped it was a sign. Maybe wisdom, the sense of what life might actually mean, touched others sometimes but it eluded her. Heroin didn't bring enlightenment; it wasn't that kind of drug.

Alicia, her eldest child, was a skinny little thing with fine, white-blonde hair and pretty blue eyes. Tracey was dark-haired and dark-eyed and Terry, the baby, was a broad-shouldered, brown-skinned toddler with green eyes. None of her kids were old enough to go to school. Kerry was swallowing Serepax to tide her over between fixes. A cocktail of chemicals that would have killed most people went down her neck. Some days she just slept. Her need for heroin increased but her income did not. She borrowed money and never paid it back, she stole things from shops and sold them. She took things from friend's houses. She took money from her mother's handbag and they had shouting matches on the phone.

'I know what you're spending it on,' her mother shouted. 'Buy those kids some bloody clothes. Buy some food.'

Her mother had given her fifty dollars that day so she moved to the phone and ordered pizza. Robbie was coming around with some stuff. The kids sat in front of the television and ate pizza while Robbie and her shot up in the front bedroom. She never shot up in front of the kids.

Some time later, she woke to hear people talking in the lounge room. She could hear their voices through the door and at first she thought she was dreaming. When she stumbled to the bedroom door and opened it, she was blinded by the light. One of the people had a piece of paper from DOCS that said they could take the kids. A blonde woman held out the piece of paper to her as she rubbed her eyes and tried to see. The blonde's skin was so white that the blue veins running from wrist to shoulder were clearly visible. Soft, white skin. Unblemished. Kerry was vaguely aware that her mother must have sent these people. Robbie was white as a ghost, staring at the syringe on the bed. He looked as if someone had carved him out of ice.

The kids were quiet, except for Alicia. 'Help, Mummy! Help, Mummy!' she called out, struggling and being carried off in the blonde woman's white arms. Her voice receded as the children were carried down the stairs and into the street.

Kerry wanted to call out to Alicia and tell her it was okay. It wasn't exactly the truth but she would've liked to call out to her all the same. It seemed like the right thing to do. Instead, she floated silently in the drug's slipstream, like a scientific specimen in a jar of ethanol. As cold and distant as a star in a crisp, dark winter sky. As lost as paradise.

The Dog That Couldn't Forget

Years ago, in the seventies, I was passing through a country town on my way to Sydney to begin a science degree at Sydney University. I was driving a ute of uncertain pedigree, as unreliable a piece of technology as was ever put together by a backyard car dealer. It consisted mostly of spares cannibalised from many other breeds of car. The dealer must have laughed himself sick as I drove it out of the car yard in Townsville.

My father shook his head when he saw it and said, 'You're not driving to Sydney in that thing?'

I only just made it into the country town and when I did, the guts, as my father would have said, fell out of the car, metaphorically speaking. I pushed it to a service station that had a repair shop and they said the repairs would take hours so I walked down Ruthven Street, turned the corner into Margaret Street and went into a pub.

Tattersall's Hotel was a shabby old place in those days. Its walls were covered in generations of colour schemes and posters for Toohey's and other beers that looked as if they had been there since the thirties. The ceiling was an interesting shade of brown from where the nicotine had created a colour scheme of its own. I ordered a VB and sat at a table with uneven legs, which moved and spilled my drink.

Then an old barfly wandered over also on spindly and unsteady legs, and sat at my table as if he knew me. 'How ya goin', mate,' he said, settling himself on a wooden chair almost as skinny as himself. 'A bloke gave me this dog once,' he said and I groaned inside. A dog story. First my car, now this.

The old man had a face that was all circles. Round eyes, round nose the colour of an over-ripe plum and a round face. He must have been in his seventies but his face had the innocent and hopeful look of a child's.

His thin, brownish-grey hair was Brylcreemed and parted on the side and in his tobacco-stained fingers the tiniest stub of cigarette sent a line of smoke straight up to add to the colour of the nicotine-painted ceiling. He was a matchstick man and his shorts would have fitted a child of ten. He was wearing old brown shoes and no socks and his checked flannelette shirt was missing a button at the top so that his bony, little chest was occasionally on display as he flicked ash and slopped his beer on the table every time he put the glass down.

'Now this dog,' he pronounced it 'dawg', 'was a lovely little animal. Part Staffordshire terrier I think she was. Her name was Tess and she was black and white and her coat sort of shone, you know. Well looked after.'

Jesus. Spare me. Make him go away.

'The fella who gave her to me was an old drunk.'

And you're not, I sneered to myself.

'Well, actually,' he puffed on the stub of cigarette, 'he sold her to me for money to buy grog. You know how it is with some people. He would've sold his mother, if you know what I mean.' He broke into a mucus-encrusted laugh that shook his bony frame so much I expected him to fall to pieces on the floor. 'Yeah, sold her to me. The poor little beggar. I took her lead and she trotted along behind me but she kept looking down the street after him.' He nodded to himself. 'They say there's no loyalty like it, you know. The loyalty of a dog for its master and this dog proved it to me once and for all. Little Tess never forgot that old drunk. Never forgot him.'

At last he stubbed the millimetre of cigarette out and looked at me brightly. 'Do you smoke, young fella?'

I had recently, foolishly, taken it up, so I flipped open the box and offered him one. 'Help yourself,' I told him. In spite of myself, I was getting interested in the dog story.

He lit the cigarette with a Redhead match and took a drag. 'Every single day of her life after that, she'd jump the fence and go downtown looking for him. I never saw him again after the night he sold her to me but she never stopped looking. She was the funniest dog I ever saw. It was like she had a human soul trapped in an animal's body. Had this look in her eye, you know what I mean? You a local?' he suddenly asked me.

'No, I'm from Townsville.'

'What brings you to our fair city?'

'Passing through. I'm going to uni. Sydney.'

'University! Well, that's the way. University of Life's all I ever went to,' he laughed again and coughed so long I feared he would die but he finally dragged a breath up from his lungs, by sheer willpower it seemed to me. Then he took a hanky out of his pocket and I prepared to abandon him, dog story and all but he only dabbed at his eyes which were watering with the strain of laughing. And of breathing.

'He used to drink at the Metropole Hotel, so she'd go and hang around there looking for him in the crowd. When she didn't find him there, she'd walk up and down Ruthven Street looking in all the shops. You probably won't believe me but she used to go into Myers and go up on the escalators, so he must've taken her up there. Must've, I reckon, cause why else would she go in there? Anyway, then she'd do the rounds of all his other haunts. The Tourist Café. The second-hand bookstores – he was a great reader, the old drunk. The things he knew! He could talk about history and stuff like that for hours. Tragic, isn't it, that someone like him could end up like that? I heard he was a teacher until he took to the bottle and they sacked him.'

He held his empty glass up and the barman pulled him another beer. I had a feeling I would be paying for it.

'She used to take off,' he said. 'So I'd drive around looking for her. When I'd find her, walking along the footpath looking at people's faces – you could see it, she was looking for him – she'd look at me with those eyes of hers. Gawd, it was such a look. Break ya heart, it would. Like she was saying, "I haven't found him." Then she'd jump up next to me on the front seat and I'd drive her home. Good thing I never married. No woman would've put up with me driving around looking for a dog all the time. I would've taken the dog back to him but he'd disappeared. No one knew where he was.'

'Did you know where he lived?'

'He had a house in Norwood Street. A timber cottage with the paint falling off it, grass never mown, gate hanging on one hinge. I heard, you know,' he leaned toward me confidentially and lowered his voice as if this was top secret, 'I heard he started drinking when his wife died. I don't know it it's true or not. She died of cancer, they say. They were both young then, no children. He never recovered.'

'He couldn't forget. Like the dog,' I said, more to myself than to him.

This thought seemed to leave the old man speechless but not for long.

'I drove there one day, to Norwood Street. Took the dog with me. She ran up the path wagging her tail and sat on the top step staring at the door while I knocked. She was smiling the way dogs do.' He shook his head. 'No one answered. I had to drag her back down the path. The place was locked up. You could tell there was no one there but she didn't want to leave. I dragged her into the car but she jumped into the back seat and watched the house out the back window as I drove away. I was sorry I took her there and I never did it again.'

The barman brought his beer and he raised the glass to me and said, 'Here's to you, young fella. Here's to your degree.'

'Thanks,' I said watching his skinny throat move as he poured the beer down.

He wiped his mouth on the back of his hand and went on. 'The last time I ever saw Tess I'd gone out looking for her in the car the way I always did but this time she saw me coming and she ducked into the crowd. I lost sight of her. I drove up and down for hours but I never found her. Never saw her again.' He was silent for a while, probably remembering how sad he'd felt that day. 'For a few weeks I went on looking. I worried about if she was eating. If she was injured somewhere. Then I realised I was acting like her. I started to think that that's why she was looking for that old drunk, because she was worried about him the way I was worried about her. Do you think a dog could feel that way?'

'I don't know,' I told him. 'There's a lot we don't know about animals.'

'Yeah,' he said, nodding his head. 'Yeah, that's right.'

I left him sitting at the table with another beer that I'd paid for.

'See ya, mate. Safe trip, eh?' he called out as I went.

Driving in the dark that night somewhere near Tenterfield, I thought about Tess the dog and the old drunk. Out there on that long straight road in the dark in my unreliable ute, I started to think about security and what it can mean. Different things to all of us. To that dog, the old drunk was security, the only security she had ever known. Watching the endless white line, I started to feel a bit strange; as if I had somehow lost my way. I started to tell myself a story about how Tess went to the Metropole Hotel one night and found the old drunk and guided him back to the house in Norwood Street in the dark. But over on the edge of the road beyond the reach of my headlights pitch black hovered and the occasional black tangle of trees seemed to be held back from the road by the barbed-wire fences. Ghosts were walking around out there. I wanted to believe she found him but I watched the dark and the dark watched me. No, it said, That's not how it was.

The Last of the Wine

When people die, they leave a lot of loose ends behind. Harry Lange had died the week before and I had been sent to 'see to his papers', as the other members of the writer's group put it.

'He wouldn't want people who aren't writers snooping in his notebooks,' Val said, grimly tossing her head.

Harry was a poet and a much better one than he would ever let himself admit. 'I'm just a hobbyist,' he would say with a dismissive grin. He was seventy-five when I joined the writers' group – old enough to be of the generation that saw poetry as unmanly. 'It's my vice,' he would say with a frightening smile. He had dentures and they belied his sweet nature, giving him the look of a small, baffled dragon.

I always enjoyed his poetry but owed him a much bigger debt. I was about thirty years younger than Harry and it was he who first mentioned that I might like to read some of Gwen Harwood's poetry.

He shyly slipped a book into my hand. 'It's only a lend,' he growled with his dragon smile.

I was not really interested but thought I'd dip into sometime. Just so I could talk to him about it if he asked. I sat at the table with a pot of coffee and some tuna sandwiches. An hour later, the coffee was stone cold and the sandwiches were uneaten. It was love at first sight.

In the introduction, Gwen Harwood was quoted as saying, 'I'm a Romantic. I am a great Romantic with all the capitals you care to give me. An upper-case Romantic…always have been…always will be.'

I found myself nodding and saying 'Yes' to my uneaten sandwiches. The shock of recognition. It was something I would have said about myself. If you find yourself saying 'No' when you're reading someone's poetry – well, that's a bad thing usually. With Gwen, it was 'Yes and yes and yes again.' How had I never heard of this woman? Well, I had, in fact. Faint memories of schooldays stirred and the English teacher with the sweet smile and greasy hair. Perhaps it was a timing thing. Understanding. Age. All of that.

> The dry reeds rustle
> And part to set the nightwind free.
> The heart holds, like remembered music,
> A landscape grown too dark to see.

Yes.

The lovers,

> Cut themselves and bleed,
> And know that knives are sharp,
> But prove with complex logic
> There's no such thing as sharpness.

Yes.

So I owed him that. When I tried to talk to him about Harwood and how her poetry had affected me, he watched me silently and only nodded from time to time.

When I realised he had said nothing for at least three minutes, I stopped and tried to apologise.

'Go on, go on,' he said. 'These things have to be said.' He showed the dragon dentures shyly.

So we became friends. I could talk any nonsense to him and he would only nod. I could rave about Harwood until he I was nearly in tears and he would never have that look that said, 'Bloody women. They're all mad.' Above all, he didn't say she was too traditional, wrote too beautifully and that I should be reading the some other poet. One of the members of the group had a complex about his age and could never be satisfied with any poem that was comprehensible. If it was also beautiful, that was simply unforgivable.

Val had said Harry had left a manuscript. A collection of his poems that they thought they could get a grant to publish. This was my mission: find the poems.

I walked up the cracked cement path which had once been red but was now an indeterminate pink. The roots of nearby trees had lifted one whole slab of cement and cracked the path. Key in hand, I approached the front door feeling strangely excited; my heart rate had quickened.

It was really quite an honour, I supposed, to be chosen to find Harry's manuscript. I was his friend, though, and it was only natural to ask me. I actually doubted there was anything to find. Harry was a great talker and he could be very convincing when he talked about poetry, especially his own. But he had been so sick for the last eighteen months of his life that I didn't expect anything approaching a publishable collection.

The front door creaked open on rusty hinges and the smell of a locked-up house rose to greet me. There was a clock ticking on a wall and a china cabinet with photos on it of a young and handsome Harry with his bride – the Joyce he often mentioned in an absent-minded way, as if she was still sitting at home (possibly knitting) waiting for his return. But Joyce had been dead for ten years. She had been a nurse and a practical, no-nonsense woman.

'Joycie didn't like poetry,' he told me once. 'She liked bridge,' he added, pulling a fearsome face that told me more than he probably really wanted me to know about their marriage. 'We didn't have any children – so she played bridge,' he sighed.

There was dust everywhere. Whenever I came over to visit him, he would always show me into the sun room at the front of the house. I had admired the tidy room and told myself he managed well for a man on his own. Now I realised that was the only room he cleaned and tidied. The bed in one room was made but a layer of dust covered everything. The bed which had obviously been Harry's was unmade. The kitchen had dishes on the draining board and in the sink, one dirty dinner plate, knife and fork and a coffee cup with coffee dregs in the bottom of it. Fungus had formed a skin across the coffee.

Down the hall was another room. It had once been a bedroom but he had moved a cheap desk in there and a swivel chair. There was a computer and a printer. I felt disappointment rise from my stomach up into my throat when I saw how dusty the desk was. Even the pens lying on it were dusty. I had wanted to be wrong but now I started to think that my belief that there was no collection of poetry was correct. Perhaps it had only ever existed in his mind.

I found his notebooks in a drawer of the desk and when I opened them I saw some indecipherable scribblings – his poems. There were five notebooks. He had dated some of the poems but lines had been scratched out, words had been written over the top of other words. Being legible wasn't one of his strong points. Then I saw some disks lying in a heap over to one side of the desk. I picked them up. Three of them had no labels but one of them had a rather grimy label, as if it had been much handled. I could hardly read the writing, of course.

'Looks like a spider crawled over the page, doesn't it?' he would laugh whenever he showed me a poem scribbled on a piece of paper. He always ended up reading it to me. He would pretend I had hurt his feelings. 'I've got a wonderful hand! Mrs Furlong caned me for blotting my copybook but that was in Grade Two!'

I took the disk over to the window and studied it carefully in the light. *The Last of the Wine: Poems 1945–1999* and, as an afterthought, in pencil he had added Harry Lange. I switched on the computer and let it go through it mechanical burping noises. Clicked on Microsoft Word and pushed in the disk. There were pages of poems but one immediately caught my attention. It was the title poem, 'The Last of the Wine'. As I read it, I could see that it was a kind of homage to Harwood's 'The Wine is Drunk' but it was in no way derivative and was full of Harry's lovely phrases and vivid images and observations. We had had a fascinating conversation about the last lines of Harwood's poem.

> My love, the light we'll wake to praise
> beats darkness to a dust of gold.

'Do you think,' I asked him, 'that she worked on those lines? Do you think she slaved over them? Or do you think it just came to her?'

'I had a friend, a Catholic priest, who used to say that God wrote all the good lines and we just got to fill in the spaces. Of course, I don't believe in God, so it put me in a rather strange position. Because you're right: lines like that do just happen. They just come, seemingly out of nowhere. My problem was that I didn't accept what he said but I had no alternative explanation. I was pretty annoyed. Of course I told him I disagreed – violently – but he could see the look on my face. A kind of guilty knowledge, I suppose.' He laughed and shook his head. 'The bugger got me that time!'

'Was he a poet?'

'He loved poetry and I'm sure he wrote it but he would never admit it.'

'It must've been his vice too.'

'It's very bad taste to mention a priest and vice in the same breath,' he said, winking.

I smiled tenderly at the memory there in that dusty room. I would miss Harry for the rest of my life and I had only just become conscious of the fact standing there staring at a computer screen and reading his poems. In 'Nightfall' Harwood had written that

> In deepest solitude we reach another's.

Yes.

'In the end, you know, we're all just shouting into the void. That's what art is.' Harry said this when he'd had too much wine but, of course, he was right. As he was right about so many things. 'I'm the best worst known poet in Australia,' he would snarl, old and drunk and comical in an armchair at the writing group's end of year Christmas party.

I would drive him home as he lay unconscious and sprawled across the back seat of the car.

I closed the computer down and took the disk out, slipped it in my pocket. I left the notebooks. No one would be able to decode them anyway. I would do everything I could to see Harry's collected poems in print. I closed the door to his study and walked out through the kitchen to the front hall. On impulse, I opened the refrigerator. There was hardly anything in there but there was a bottle of red wine, almost empty. Looking at the wine, I realised how much I wanted Harry to wake to that light that beat darkness to a dust of gold. Amen to that, I thought. With a sacramental gesture, I hoisted the bottle and drank the last of the wine in a gulp. Superstitiously I hoped it was a sign. 'Amen to that!' I shouted into the silent house.

It was winter and when I walked back down the cracked path, darkness was already closing in. Two young lovers walked past, their laughter echoing down the empty street. They had their arms around each other. I could only hope that Harry had found some light / beyond that field of black everlasting flowers. Amen to that too.

Roads and Cliffs

My sister was driving us up to the north coast of Queensland to the newly built villas where she was holidaying but she made it clear that we could only stay three days. It was four days to Christmas and her friend was coming. He was a married man, an accountant – as she was. I didn't have the money to stay at Seashells Resort but Clare did and she was always generous. She had no husband and no children. When I was feeling frustrated and bitchy, I would think to myself, She can afford to be generous. She's got money to burn. I wasn't feeling that way, though, on that sunny day, zipping along the motorway in her silver-grey Mercedes. I lease it, she always said to those crass enough to ask. It's a tax write-off.

I had been married a long time before my marriage ended. I learned to be dependent and old habits die hard. The strain of a bad marriage destroys a lot of things: self-confidence, for example. I was struggling to get mine back.

My ten-year-old son Danny sat in the back of the smooth, padded, air-conditioned car. Our own car rattled and was only air-conditioned when a strong breeze blew.

'It's a shame you can't stay longer, Kate,' Clare was saying, 'but my friend is coming. He was actually supposed to come up yesterday but something happened and he couldn't get away.'

I didn't say anything. I wondered if his wife knew. I wondered if he and his wife had quarrelled. Or if it was some family crisis. A child with mumps or chickenpox. Then the Glasshouse Mountains were silhouetted against the cloudless sky.

I smiled and turned to my son, 'Look at that mountain, Danny. Can you see it? It looks like a pyramid.'

He scanned the horizon. 'Yes, I can see it!' He pressed his face against the window. He was mad about Egypt. He had a collection of pyramids at home on a shelf over his desk.

'That's your favourite of the Glasshouse Mountains isn't it, Clare?'

I turned to my sister and the misery she was feeling leapt at me. Her mouth was sad. Then she smiled but her fingers drummed on the wheel.

'Yep. I like that one. Different to the rest.' She was thinking about her married lover.

We got to Seashells Resort around four in the afternoon. I could see that the sun still baked the ground even though the shadows were lengthening. The villas were cool ice cream colours, each one topped with a tower outlined in contrasting pastel greens, blues and yellows. As we drove down the smooth, paved central driveway to the two-storey villa, the sea was suddenly there at the bottom of the hill; so vast, unknowable and untamed that it took my breath away. The first sight of it was like diving into it. A thrilling, cool blueness filled my eyes all the way to the horizon.

My son undid his seatbelt, jumped to his feet and yelled, 'Look, Mum! Look! It's the road to the sea.'

I laughed, reached back and ruffled his hair.

Clare smiled. 'Looks like it, doesn't it?' she said, expertly guiding the Merc into the car port of number 16.

We lugged our bags in and understated luxury greeted us. Pale beige carpets, sea-blue couches, white doors and a sliding glass door led to a balcony. From the glass door the sea seemed close enough to touch. Restless and glittering with light and shadow playing across it while little, foam-capped waves spun across its surface.

Danny dropped the bags he was carrying. 'Wow! Can we go to the beach?'

'Tomorrow,' I told him. He wasn't allowed to go to the beach on his own and I wasn't in the mood to go and neither was Clare. One day he would go to the beach on his own, as an adult with all the virtues and vices of a free man but that was a long way off. I would think about that some other time.

'We'll go along the nature walk.' Clare threw open the sliding door to the balcony, letting in the sound of the sea and turned on a ceiling fan. 'It'll be fun. There's some cliffs but it's okay as long as you stay away from the edge.'

I expected her to laugh but she didn't. Had she forgotten, I wondered? Had she forgotten my fear of heights? There was a cold feeling on the back of my neck and a thin film of sweat above my upper lip. I saw my body falling down to be smashed on the rocks. I saw Danny falling. Then I despised myself. I wouldn't be a coward. I wouldn't be defeated by fear. I had been, for too long. I wasn't going to let my fearless, independent sister feel contempt for me.

That night, Clare ordered in a classy chicken pizza from a local restaurant and opened a bottle of Veuve Cliquot. For dessert there was lemon-flavoured sorbet. Everything was delicious and after a glass of champagne my tension melted away. I knew it would be back. It was a habit too. My husband had disapproved of almost everything I said or did. His attitude created a lot of tension and it had become a part of me. When I realised, at last, that his disapproval was never going to go away there was no way back from the realisation. I didn't leave for another year but my marriage really ended the day he looked at me with contempt once too often. I was always stubborn.

'You and Danny getting on okay?' Clare broke into my thoughts.

Danny was already asleep in his plush green and cream bedroom.

I hesitated. Were we? 'Oh, yeah. It's hard but we're getting there.'

Her brown eyes studied me as if I was a page of figures that didn't add up. 'You'll be okay. You should have left him years ago,' she said dispassionately. 'You gave him every chance. He was a bit of a sad case. I always thought so but you couldn't accept any criticism of him.'

'That was because I knew he was a sad case too.'

High on champagne and the moment, we giggled.

'Is your friend…?'

'A sad case?'

'No, no not that. I mean is he good to you?'

Her face gave nothing away. 'As good as he can be, I suppose. It's not easy.'

We both knew what she meant. A man's wife and children always get in the way of romancing his mistress.

We took our champagne out on to the balcony. The ocean advanced and retreated out in the darkness and the lights twinkled in a narrow strip along the foreshore. We sat at the table and sipped the cold champagne in the still, muggy night air.

'Once I would have thought this was success,' Clare laughed.

'Isn't it?'

'Success is overrated. Nothing's painless.' She stared out over the sea.

'I always thought success would be an anaesthetic.'

'Well, that's just a lie. I believed it too. Remember that religion book at school?'

'The Catechism?'

'Yeah. Wasn't the devil called "The Father of all Lies" in there?' Clare snorted with laughter.

'It's no laughing matter, miss,' I told her and the memory of Sister Philomena, fat, dim and hopelessly good, made us both laugh so much we could hardly breathe.

The last thing I thought about before I went to sleep was the walk along the cliffs.

Breakfast next morning was eaten on the balcony with the ever-moving sea as a backdrop. The sea was in light and sparkling aspect, young and sprightly as a child. A child on holiday – as Danny, in fact. I smiled to myself and told myself to stop being fatuous but I couldn't feel bad about anything. There was no husband staring at me, waiting for my next mistake. I felt myself exhale and realised I'd been holding my breath for years. I watched Danny spooning up mango, banana and yoghurt. We lingered at the table in the early morning coolness, all three of us hardly speaking but completely at ease with each other.

By ten o'clock it was hot and humid but Clare was determined we would have our nature walk so I dressed in a black swimsuit, buttoned on a wrap-around floral skirt and pulled on a light white cotton top. On my head I wore a big straw hat with white flowers around the brim and flat, black sandals on my feet.

Danny was bouncing up and down with excitement. 'Come on, come on. I'm ready.'

'Wear your cap. Go and get it.'

He ran off to find it.

Clare looked glamorous in a filmy purple dress that stopped well above her knees and white sneakers and socks. She wore a black cap. She always looked good. Freedom and money. That was her secret.

'Are you going to have a swim?' I asked her and she lifted the dress to reveal tanned thighs and a lime-green swimsuit.

'Of course. We'll all need a swim after our walk to cool off.'

We drove to the beach and parked. Soon we were walking single file down a track of soft sand, feeling the sun stinging our skin and listening to the buzz of cicadas. After a while, every bit of shade was a luxury, more precious than gold or diamonds. We panted in the sun and heaved sighs of relief in the shade. Then I realised that the track had led us steadily closer to the cliff. Far below, I could see rocks and the foaming, clawing waves. A ridiculous guard rail, barely knee-high, was all that stood between the walker and death. My stomach tightened and my mouth went dry. I couldn't close my eyes but I tried to close my mind. I only thought about moving forward, about walking. Mercifully the section of track near the cliffs was very short.

I looked back at Danny and smiled shakily but he looked a bit alarmed at my smile so I stopped. His face was flushed with the humidity and the uphill part of the walk but we were soon going downhill and entered an area of shade. I felt giddy and panicky, though, because I could see another section of trail close to the cliffs ahead of us. Falling to my death in front of Danny would scar him for life. That thought saved me. My legs felt like jelly but I looked straight ahead at the soft sand beneath my feet and pretended there were no cliffs.

After, you have to walk back again, I suddenly thought, and that thought almost paralysed me but I knew I had to go on to have that cool swim in the sea which I was now longing for. Sweat trickled down my back and the thought of a cool swim made it possible to keep moving towards that section of track that ran close to the edge of the cliff. No guard rail at all this time. It lasted seconds but I felt extreme fear and extreme fear is very unpleasant. For the first time, I knew Clare was watching me but I turned my frightened face to her as if to say Yes, I'm scared to death but I won't turn back. I marched on.

After what seemed like hours but couldn't have been more than twenty minutes, we emerged from the bush beside a rough concrete ramp that led down to the beach.

'Look, Danny,' I called to him, light-headed with relief that I could relax for the moment, 'it's the road to the sea.'

Danny looked at the concrete ramp, and then placed his feet on it with a small boy's arrogance. 'Nah,' he called over his shoulder as he launched himself down it. 'This isn't it.'

Clare and I followed him at a jog and I thought to myself, Which road is the road to the sea? Or to Xanadu? Or to wisdom? At school I always knew the answers. It drove everyone else in the class crazy.

We stripped our clothes off, laughing and falling over in the sand. Then we hit the ocean running and were knocked down and dragged back on to the beach in a huge wave. I swallowed a lot of salt water because I was laughing when I fell. We splashed around for an hour or so and I felt the tension of the walk and all my fear washing away in the ocean. The cradle of life. The Great Healer.

The walk back to the car was hot and exhausting but strangely easy. I felt as if I'd used up all my fear. The sandy track was almost pleasant to the foot.

Two days later, Clare put us on a bus for our trip back. Her friend had called. There was a chance he could get away for a couple of days. Sitting on the bus with Danny near a window so he could say goodbye to the sea, I looked at my sister dutifully waiting to wave goodbye. I wanted to yell for everyone to hear, 'You're a class act, Clare. I love you.' I didn't. I smiled inanely through the glass and she smiled back and waved a tanned hand. As the bus negotiated the narrow road to the highway, I looked back and saw her, a lone figure, walking to her car. Her friend might come, he might not. She would chill the wine and wait. Life gave no guarantees. She didn't ask for any.

'Bye, sea,' Danny said, waving and smiling a half-foolish smile. 'Bye. See you next time.'

Soon he would believe such things were beneath him. Sooner than I cared to think, he would be on his own road to the sea and I wouldn't be able to walk it with him.

For a long time, he was quiet and I saw that he was staring out the window.

'You're quiet. What are you thinking?'

'Nothing. I'm waiting to see the pyramid. It's one of the Seven Wonders of the World, you know.'

I looked at his smooth dark head and his serious brown eyes.

'And love is the eighth,' I told him.

He didn't sneer and he didn't look embarrassed, he just nodded. All children know that this is true. I had forgotten it until that moment.

The Settlement: AD 2032

Colorado

The Vanks were dying like flies that summer. Business was booming. I got paid fifty dollars for every body I collected. No one cared if they died – at least no one in authority cared – but the bodies had to be collected and burned, otherwise diseases from the rotting corpses could jump out of the Settlement and spread to everyone else. No one in the Settlement was capable of finding their feet to put their shoes on let alone moving all those bodies.

My name is Colorado and my wife's name is Wyoming. Two of the most popular names on the legal names list. I saw President James on TV last night saying that the menace of drugs was now under control in Australia. Even in his wildest fantasies he doesn't believe that.

When I came downstairs to breakfast that morning, Wyoming was sitting there with that look on her face.

'What's wrong?' I asked her.

'I feel like shit.'

'What's new?'

'That's what I need. Encouragement…'

'If you overdose just once more, I don't know if I'll be able to keep you out of the Settlement. They'll report you next time at the hospital. They won't have any choice. Stay away from that stuff. If you feel bad, drink some Scotch.'

'That stuff's poison. You know what it does to my liver.'

She was straight-faced. I couldn't tell if she was being ironic or not. Wyoming is dark and pretty with short hair like a little boy's and very small ears. I love her but she's a weak vessel. A frail, ethereal girl who's come back from the dead twice and who carries the shadow world in her eyes, in her thin, white hands, in her hypersensitive body language.

It's the children in the Settlement that upset me the most. When we drive in there to take the bodies out (all used up and with other, ravaged junkies standing around), well, I've hardened myself to that but sometimes there's a kid or a couple of kids standing there and you know it's their mother or their father, sister or brother or some protector they've attached themselves to who's gone and died and left them to fend for themselves. Kids like that are supposed to be taken out of the Settlement but it only happens if some relative kicks up a stink. Then they go in and take them out. I try not to think about the ones that are still in there.

I know Wyoming's still doing all kinds of drugs but it's smack that will get her taken to the Settlement. When she's being honest with me, she tells me there's no substitute for that sweet hit. Not sex, not God, not me, not nothin'. She usually says these things when we're poisoning our livers with Scotch. I've never used heroin but some of the people who got off it tell me that anyone who's on it is either sick or about to be sick. I don't see the attraction myself. But then I wouldn't, would I?

'At least I don't use cocaine.' Wyoming smiles and shrugs like a child.

'You can't afford cocaine. Only members of parliament can afford cocaine.'

Driving along later in the green sanitation truck (that's what the government calls them; the junkies in the Settlement call them green meanies) I could still see the smile she gave me when I made the joke about cocaine: proud, distant yet completely into it, like a bee burrowing into a nectar-drenched flower. I loved her.

Wyoming

They put people like me in the Settlement. It's nothing personal, they say, but you're a threat. I see their point. Colorado is so straight and I love him for it but it makes me angry too. He's my sanity. I say that even though it's too much to ask, for someone to be my sanity. The government spouts regurgitated Marx but they say they are capitalists. If I still gave a shit,

I'd be confused. From each according to their ability, to each according to their needs. Someone like me produces nothing, of course, so I get nothing, or would get nothing if Colorado didn't feed me. They call this their manifesto, the jerks.

Jimmy Perkins, whose legal name was Kansas but who always called himself Jimmy, said this manifesto was an excuse to hurt others. 'Invented by sadists to protect them from their victim's revenge,' he'd say.

He's been dead five years now. Hard to believe. Died raving in the Settlement, they say, but you can't believe anything you hear. You can believe those sad, little pen-pushers in parliament house least of all. They've never seen what I've seen – great sheets of purple light moving through a room on feet of fire while the universe moved like some marvellous machine and I watched it move. I've heard colours singing oh so divine. That's why I'm a threat. Nothing can be the same after. Life is grey and that other place is so inviting. LSD is the drug they should fear but you don't go to the Settlement for using it.

Heroin's the one. Makes slaves of people, they say, but what they mean is, we want you to be our slaves instead. Chained to the wheel. Mass production. Mass media. Mass conformity. I don't want to go to the Settlement. They feed you; they even give you cigarettes! You get a place to live – it's all paid for by the government. Aids was rampant once but it looked too bad, even though it was killing the addicts off very effectively. So those hypocrites sent people in to hand out clean needles. It's a terrible place, though, and everyone knows it. People have been known to kill themselves with an overdose to avoid going in there, where they're going to die anyway.

The junkies are called Vanks, short for vanquished. Australians love nicknames and as President James preached in his famous preachment, 'These are the vanquished.' The pompous clown. Don't I know every time I look at him or hear him speak that he was born vanquished and will die that way? He's got a lot to answer for. I've even heard that he likes little boys. I heard that he gets them from the Settlement and that made my blood run cold until someone told me that he sends them to school like little male concubines and I decided that they might be better off. How do you choose between evil and evil? I've never been a pragmatist. A flaw in my character. I'm actually a very moral person. That side of me annoys Colorado a bit because he thinks he's made his peace with all of it. He does what he has to do and if he didn't, where would I be? Morals come at a price and he's the one who pays.

Colorado

'I have a theory,' Prairie said, throwing his cigarette out the window of the truck. 'I think all those junkies were once the unemployed. Sitting around all day they dabbled in drugs – too much free time, nothing meaningful to do, you know. Then there were fewer and fewer jobs and more and more drugs. They started to steal stuff, doing break and enters and all that. That's the real reason they put them in the Settlement: they were knocking off the burghers' goods. There were never going to be any jobs, so they locked 'em up. Make sense to you, Colorado?'

'Everything you say makes sense.' I gave him a grin.

His theory was what I had believed for a long time. Capitalists don't care about anything but capital – which is only logical. You had to be careful what you said or who you said it to, but Prairie was my friend. We trusted each other.

I turned the truck towards the settlement. A short distance away was the newest in nuclear reactors, so the Vanks were zapped by radiation as well as heroin on a regular basis. That, at least, was another of my theories. The government denied it of course and since the reactor stood halfway between a primary school and the Settlement it was democratic, I suppose. The snotty-nosed little kids in the Settlement got their dose and the little blue bloods in the private primary school got theirs. At all schools, capitalist principles were taught but prayer was forbidden.

'Their allegiance is to the government and to the government alone. We, as a society, cannot afford the luxury of a spiritual life,' Prez James had said in tones of phony regret. 'Fate has no favourites' was another of his favourite sayings. He and his merry men and women seemed constantly to disprove that one.

'Wasn't the settlement supposed to fix crime?' Prairie asked of no one in particular.

'Yeah. So?'

'It's a hellhole of crime in there, you know. The guy in charge of distributing drugs is running black market heroin on the side. Women selling themselves and their kids to get it, so I've heard. Where do you think all those bodies come from?'

'Natural wastage. Overdoses.'

'You've seen the bodies. They're murdering each other in there. Fighting over drugs and money just like they did on the outside. Ever had a good look at the wire fence around the place?'

'What about it?'

'It's electrified.'

'Is it?'

'Yep. Hardly anyone on the outside knows. The Vanks know but who're they gonna tell? Everyone hates them. Everyone's scared of them. No one cares.'

I said nothing.

'I've picked up bodies they've obviously taken off the fence. Suicides probably. Burns all over them…'

'Look, Prairie, do you have to? Can't we just…?'

'Okay. Forget I spoke.'

Silence.

I said, 'What's all this leading to?'

'I've heard a rumour.'

'You're always hearing rumours.'

'Untrue, Colorado,' he laughed. 'Anyway, you know my rumours are always true.'

'Why is that?'

'Because they come from high up.' Here he pointed at the roof of the truck. 'That's why.'

'Sleeping with a senator?'

'Not quite.' A wink and a lascivious grin. 'The government's scared of the situation out in the Settlement. They've lost control. The guards are on the take and word is a nasty storm is brewing.'

I laughed. 'What's that mean? The Vanks going to overpower the guards with their body odour?'

I thought I was very funny but Prairie didn't laugh.

'Think about it! What weapon do these poor bastards have?'

Slowly a syringe evolved into view on the monitor of my mind.

'Syringes?'

'Bingo, amigo. Syringes. And heroin. Lots of it.'

'What're you talking about?'

'Rebellion, Col, rebellion. Some might even call it a revolution.'

I laughed again. Mostly in disbelief. I didn't think it was funny any more. 'Who've you been talking to?' I asked him.

'Someone high up.'

'God?' I sneered. I was annoyed. I didn't want to know. I just wanted to do my job, make money and keep Wyoming safe. 'I don't want to hear any more, Prairie. Leave me out of it.'

'You have to turn left up here.'

'I know that,' I snapped.

When I looked at him, he was nodding and smiling. Later, I knew that he'd been trying to warn me. He'd done the best he could but it was already too late to leave me out of it.

A Man Called Lucifer

The man who would lead the Vanks in their uprising was named Texas but he had renamed himself Lucifer. Hardly anyone remembered the old meaning. The professors in Coca Cola University would have known but no one asked them anything these days. They dressed up in their academic robes the way clowns dress up for the circus and handed out degrees that had been paid for the way anything else was paid for. Coffee, whisky, headache tablets – or an economics degree. Take your pick. Choose your poison. The professors were shunned these days as revisionist backsliders always secretly longing for the days when universities weren't just edfactories, churning out cannon fodder for the dollar war, the yen war, the euro war.

Being a revisionist backslider was the only thing that still approximated to a sin in a society that couldn't afford the luxury of a spiritual life. Someone had told Texas that Lucifer meant 'light' and he liked the sound of it.

'I'll make them fall,' he muttered to himself. 'I'll make them fall. Buckets of blood,' he muttered. 'Buckets of blood.'

Lucifer had had no heroin for a month. Though he still collected it from the centre every day. He stockpiled heroin and syringes waiting for the moment to strike. There were twenty who had joined him. They called themselves 'triumphalists' as an antidote to the despised name others had given them – the vanquished.

Lucifer had done a lot of drugs and his brain was like an almost burned-out fuse. It sparked only fitfully but he knew quite a lot. He'd seen them take his son Salem away and everyone knew where those little boys went. That day he cried for the first time in years. The next day he stopped using. He shivered, he vomited, he doubled up in pain but he persisted. He'd sit with a photo of Salem's mother in his hand. She'd died of an overdose when Salem was four. In Lucifer's burnt-out brain there was only one thought: kill President James and get his son back.

Today was the day. Rubicon, he thought. He liked the sound of the word but he couldn't remember what it meant. He turned it over in his mind like a jewel. Whatever it meant, he decided that it was a good word. An important word.

Wyoming

Sitting on the bed, I watched the colours. So beautiful. I looked at my hand and power radiated out of it. I was safe and warm and back in my mother's womb. Out the window I could see a hill dotted with little houses; then this old man peeped over the top of it. After a while, I realised it was my grandfather. He'd been dead for twenty years but he was huge and smiling. I smiled back. Then he stood up and cast a gigantic shadow over the hill. I could hear shouting and screaming somewhere very, very far away. My grandfather strode off into the distance, his head almost bumping the sun. This was great acid. It just exploded. Rivulets of knowledge seemed to trickle through my veins. My bed became a boat. I drifted away, my feet dangling over the edge of the bed, into the cool, cool water.

When the green meanie pulled in, Lucifer and the others moved cautiously towards it.

'Where are the bodies?' Colorado said, thinking they were there to put the bodies on the truck.

'There'll be bodies,' a grizzled old man growled. 'Oh yes, there'll be bodies for sure,' and Colorado noticed the barrel of the gun that the old man held for the first time. In wonder, suddenly understanding everything, Colorado turned to Prairie and saw that he was handing out guns. 'You said syringes,' was all he could find to say. He felt dazed and frightened. This was big. And treasonous.

'We're not gonna waste good shit on these bastards,' Lucifer grunted, taking aim at a guard leaning on a wall in the sun doing some deal with a dirty, bedraggled junkie who smiled toothlessly, idiotically at his persecutor. Lucifer dropped the guard with one shot. 'Rubicon,' he shouted. 'It's destiny.'

'We're saving the smack for privileged members of the community,' the grizzled old man laughed and showed his rotting teeth.

'What's going on with these laughing loons? What is this?' The blood was pounding in Colorado's brain.

'It's called a coup, brother,' Prairie told him. 'Go home and look after Wyoming. The army's on the move in the city and they can't rule out collateral damage.'

'Who's behind this?'

'Who do you think?'

'The rumourmonger?'

'Good name for her.' Prairie laughed excitedly, his eyes glittered. 'She's taking over from James. It's been planned for a long time.'

'Who is she?'

'James's wife. We're what you might call friends.'

'His wife?'

'You must've heard about his habits. A woman can only take so much.'

Prairie pulled a face. 'Don't feel sorry for him. He's a bastard. He'll be given a fair trial before they execute them. The army's backing his wife.'

Colorado just stood. The men with guns scattered, firing as they ran and setting the junkie's nerves atwitter. Most of them disappeared into their wrecked government housing, their children on their heels.

'Take the truck, get out of here.' Prairie gave him a push. He handed Colorado a card. 'Keep this on you at all times.'

Colorado hastily stuck the card in his pocket.

As he drove out the now unguarded gates, he glanced in the rear-view mirror and saw Prairie firing at people he couldn't see. Wyoming would be off her face, probably in the upstairs bedroom. He hoped she was asleep and not weaving around at a window where she would probably get shot.

'Please,' he prayed to the God he didn't believe in. 'Please don't let her get hurt.'

Colorado

I ran up the stairs stumbling and calling her name. She was lying on the bed and she was still, so still. I said her name again and her eyes flickered, then opened. She took a breath as deep as a newborn baby's and I had tears in my eyes. She was looking straight at me, still asleep, vague and lovely and lost. I wanted to say, 'I love you, Wyoming. You're the love of my life,' but I said nothing – just drank her in with my eyes. Then I lay down beside her and held her, which after all was what I lived for. I'm a simple man with simple needs.

I couldn't remember falling asleep but I woke from a hideous nightmare of deserts and carrion bones and saw that Wyoming still slept soundly. I looked at my watch and saw it was midnight, the witching hour.

I found the card Prairie had given me and on it I read, 'Prairie Teller, Commander in Chief, Australian Armed Forces, dual code Z222111.'

Gibberish. I could picture Prairie with his blond curls and his angelic face, having these cards printed by another of the revolutionaries. His serious young face as the little cards popped out one by one. What was the saying? Nothing is true but that believing makes it so. I thought that Prairie was probably already dead.

Then I turned on the television in the middle of a newsflash. I watched in disbelief as Prairie and a blonde woman I assumed to be James's wife faced a bank of microphones and a wall of flashing cameras. I turned up the sound.

'Today,' the woman said, 'there was an incident in the Settlement…'

I was amazed. But the card had some value after all and that was good news. I opened a window and studied the night sky with its sprinkling of stars. I sniffed. The odour of smoke and death still hung in the air, and I wondered what the new day would bring. I wanted only two things. That Wyoming would live and go on being my wife and that we would not live in interesting times. I put the card carefully away in my wallet. I had a hunting knife. I found it and put it under my pillow before I lay down next to Wyoming. I wouldn't sleep but if anyone wanted to hurt her that night, they would have to kill me first.

The Weeping Madonna

Peppertree was a pretty, ordinary little country town west of the Great Dividing Rang until the Madonna started weeping. Population 542, a church, a school, a service station, a bank (closed), a library, a grocery store, a pub a church hall and the police station – a weatherboard house with high steps leading up to the front door. There was also Clarry, the town drunk. That's how it all began.

Constable David Jenkins, lone custodian of law and order in Peppertree, had to arrest old Clarry, who'd gone mad out in the bush in the tin shed he called home. Clarry drank whatever came to hand. Cheap plonk, good whisky on pension day and, just before pension day, metho. Clarry had an old rifle that he would brandish at anyone who came on his land – it was a local joke. No one actually thought it could fire until that night. It could. It was a relic so it couldn't fire straight but when Clarry drove into town that night in his ute, bullets whistled through the air and people hit the ground and stayed there. Clarry, his eyes red as a demon's from hell, took aim at anything that moved and some things that didn't.

Alerted to Clarry's shooting spree, Jenkins ran down the main street and saw Clarry staggering in the direction of St Michael's church. He gave chase, cautiously. He knew a stray bullet would kill him just as effectively as one that was meant to hit him. He saw Clarry open the large, wooden church doors.

Father Johnson was one of the old school who refused to lock the doors of the church. 'The House of Gahd', as he called it, was a long, timber building with crucifixes at either end of its pitched roof.

As he reached it, the church door slammed shut in Jenkins's face.

'Shit,' he muttered, 'now it's a siege.'

The shopkeeper Bill Blocksedge, the publican Ray Hanna and Father Johnson materialised out of the night.

'Go through the sacristy, lad,' Father Johnson whispered. 'He won't be expecting you. Not from that direction.'

'We'll stay here and if he comes out we'll grab him.' Bill Blocksedge nodded enthusiastically as if agreeing with himself.

'Yeah, we'll hide near the front door,' Ray Hanna added.

'Okay,' Jenkins whispered back and crept off in the moonlight to the small side door that led to the sacristy.

As he tiptoed across the sacristy floor, he heard snoring. It got louder as he came out on to the altar and he saw Clarry asleep at the feet of a large statue of the Madonna, snoring fit to wake the dead. Jenkins tiptoed over to him and gently removed the relic of a firearm from Clarry's hands. He didn't wake. All four men then carried Clarry out of the church and put him in the police car. He slept soundly all the way to the police house but when the car stopped, he woke like a recalcitrant baby and started yelling at the top of his voice.

'Cockroaches!' he bawled. 'They're green. They're green. They're going to eat me!'

'Yeah, yeah, Clarry. Calm down.'

'Cockroaches! Cockroaches!' Clarry raved.

Jenkins dragged him out of the car and wrestled him to the lock-up behind the house. Placed in the cell, Clarry passed out again. Jenkins put him in the S position so he wouldn't choke on his own vomit, locked the door and made his weary way back to his bed and his anxious wife.

'It's okay,' he whispered to her. 'Just old Clarry. He's drunk.'

She mumbled sleepily into her pillow.

No need to tell her about the gun. Soon the police house was silent. It occupants slept. The man in the lock-up wandered from one terrifying nightmare to another.

Next morning when Father Johnson arrived to celebrate Mass, he noticed the change that had come over the statue of the Madonna. 'Mother of God,' he whispered, staring at the Virgin's face. He blinked several times and made the sign of the cross.

Venice Belmont was on the run from the father of her children. The old green Holden she drove bumped along the highway through a parched landscape. It hadn't rained in Peppertree country for many a long month. Venice didn't much care, though. She didn't care where she took her kids as long as Kevin couldn't find them. Or her. She looked in the rear-view mirror at the goodbye gift he'd given her, the purple-yellow bruise on her face. She glanced at the mark of his fingers on her arm, etched in the same yellow purple. Venice was a tough girl and she'd had a tough life but she decided her kids deserved better. With Kevin and her, it was different. They would have fought it out to the end if it hadn't been for the kids. That was the kind of relationship they had.

The kids had fought and cried for the first half of the trip. It nearly made her crazy but not so crazy that she thought about turning the car around. Now they slept. Toby had a tear-stained face, streaked with dirt. He was four. Talitha was eight and Merry was six. Poor little buggers, she thought. I haven't given you much of a life. It's all going to be different now, though. A new beginning in Queensland.

Venice was twenty-six. She and Kevin had met at a wild party when her parents were away. They'd had sex under the pool table. She was fourteen and it was the first time for her. He'd lost interest after that and they didn't get back together until she was eighteen. He got her pregnant. They'd been together ever since.

How could anything that seemed so fated be so mistaken? So poisonous. Perhaps the powerful attraction that had drawn them together was generated by the fact that they were allergic to each other. Perhaps she'd done something terrible in a former life. She laughed softly and bitterly to herself and flicked straight hair the colour of straw out of her eyes. Her eyes were green like a cat's. She weighed seven and a half stone and stood five feet four but she felt as if life had decided that she was built for burdens or as those Americans on talk shows were always saying, 'Challenges'.

She saw the sign that said 'Welcome to Peppertree', hesitated and then turned off the highway and went in the direction that the sign pointed.

Meanwhile, there was consternation in Father Johnson's church and indeed in Father Johnson himself. He was no Jesuit. He was a simple man of simple faith. Of course he'd heard of this phenomenon in other places and he racked his brain for explanations. Wasn't it said in one place, Italy he thought, that it was glue or condensation – things like that? Pushing away any superstitious thoughts, he reached for a soft cloth he saw lying on a cupboard (left by the ladies who cleaned the church, he supposed) and ventured out on to the altar. He stared at the statue of the Virgin. Then he reached up with the cloth and dabbed at her eyes. Whatever it was, it seemed to be gone. It was probably just a trick of the light.

He took the cloth back to the sacristy and began laying out his vestments for Mass. Only fifty or so worshippers ever turned up but it was better they hadn't seen it.

Halfway through Mass, as he stood in the pulpit giving his sermon, he heard whispering. Hardly perceptible at first and then quite loud. The altar boy was staring. Father Johnson hardly dared look behind him at the state of the statue but finally turned with a kind of resignation to look at what had transfixed his parishioners. The Madonna was weeping again. Summoning a ferocious look, he cleared his throat. Loudly. Then he went on with his sermon, daring his congregation to whisper, to point or to bring the inexplicable tears on the Virgin's face to his attention in any way whatsoever. There was a rational explanation, he was sure of that. Later, in the peace and quiet of the presbytery, he would remember what it was.

In the car on the way home from Mass, Claire Jenkins turned to her husband and said, 'Did you see those tears on Our Lady's face? What do you think it meant?'

Constable Jenkins paused but only briefly before deciding his position. 'What tears?' he asked.

'Didn't you see them?'

'I didn't see anything.'

'The Madonna was weeping.'

He gave a short laugh and started the car. 'Don't be silly. Stop fooling around in the back, you two,' he told his children.

They stopped.

Then Gerard said to Kate. 'Why was Our Lady crying?'

Kate shrugged. 'How would I know?'

Kate was six, two years younger than her brother, and she knew her limitations. Their parents exchanged a glance. Then they drove home in silence. Neither parent considered it strange that though they believed in God, a supernatural being who knew everything and was all-powerful, they found themselves incredulous at a few tears on a statue's face. If God truly was God, then this would be child's play for him. The equivalent of reading the Grade One primer.

Venice Belmont needed a place to stay and since there was no real estate office in Peppertree, she decided that the grocery store was the place to go. In these towns, the grocer knew everything. She only knew about country towns from what she'd seen in Australian films. She was a city girl herself.

Bill Blocksedge almost stood to attention when she walked in. He even sucked in his gut. He thought she looked like a pop singer. He knew she was no local. 'Hello, love,' he cooed. 'How can I help you?'

She was used to this kind of attention from men, though she hated her freckles and had no idea that she was beautiful. Kevin had encouraged her in this mistake whenever possible. Sometimes he made her stand in front of a mirror while he told her how ugly she was and how no other man would ever want her. She didn't care about that now, though. A man was the last thing she needed. One of her friends had told her once that if there were twenty men in a room she would pick the one that was exactly wrong for her. She believed it now.

She was still young, though she felt ancient sometimes. She still hoped for happiness. She wasn't bitter or cynical. When she left, she'd taken Kevin's stash of drug money. He always told her she was stupid and he must have believed it. Why else would he leave ten thousand dollars in a plastic bag in the toilet cistern when she knew where it was? She'd paid three thousand dollars for the Holden, peeling the notes off like a bank robber spending the loot. She thought the dealer gave her a funny look and as she drove out of the car yard he was on the phone. He was in Sydney, though. Another state, another life away.

The kids were caterwauling now, tired out. She struggled to fit the huge, old-fashioned key into the lock. She'd paid a month's rent, straight off. She needed a month to pull herself together. She opened the door and the kids trooped in. Yes. She liked it. People had been happy in this house, she could feel it straight away. Nothing fancy but clean and tidy and full of bits of old-fashioned furniture. She hated modern furniture. She was a romantic and she felt was at home as soon as she stepped through the door. After running a bath for her hungry, sleepy brood, she got them fed and in their pyjamas. The long drive had tired them out. They slept. Venice sat in the silent old house, sipped a cup of coffee at the scrubbed pine table and smoked her last cigarette. She knew that later she would wake in the darkness and sit up in terror. She'd left Kevin before.

Stories about the weeping Madonna started to spread and Peppertree seemed to change from one day to the next. The town boomed. A man who'd grown up there came back to visit his widowed mother and was amazed. Pilgrims by the busload constantly arrived and departed. Souvenir shops sprang up all down the main street. Someone built a coffee shop on the small river that always managed to exist even when it didn't rain for years and Venice got a job there as a waitress. It was called The Grotto, an allusion to the Madonna's miraculous appearance in a cave. Some people said it was at Fatima, others that it was at Lourdes. The business people who had descended on the town counted their money and didn't speculate. Religion was not their area of expertise. Land prices soared and soon there was a real estate office in the main street. There was even talk of opening a convention centre to house the ever-bigger prayer meetings the pilgrims attended.

Peppertree's church now had security guards and Father Johnson was forever telling them to get out from under his feet. The business people who had moved into town insisted on them. Suppose the statue was stolen or vandalised? What would happen to their investment? Father Johnson would sometimes dream that he was back in the days before the Madonna started weeping and wake up happy.

One day, Venice woke with a bad feeling. She couldn't explain it. She almost got into an argument with some supercilious yuppies who had come to Peppertree to take a look at the Bible-bashers and the renecks. Two men and two women. They looked Venice up and down, took in her western suburbs blonde-slut hair, skin-tight black jeans, scuffed black boots, her cycle-slut make-up. They exchanged furtive smiles and studied the menu.

One of the men, a bull-necked ex-rugby forward, sneered, 'This town's enough to make a virgin weep.'

'How can people be taken in? It's such an obvious hoax. It's medieval,' one of the women, a thirtyish brunette was saying as Venice collected their menus.

'How can be people be so gullible?' one of the other women murmured.

After their first scornful appraisal, they now preferred to pretend that Venice didn't exist. She retreated into fantasy. 'Maybe you should ask yourselves why the Madonna's crying,' she pictured herself saying to them, Maybe she's heard about Rwanda. Simmering like a slow cooking casserole, she imagined their startled faces snapping to attention while she walked away throwing a professional smile over her shoulder.

When the yuppies left, they gave her a five-dollar tip. Venice smiled, tight-lipped, but she took the money. She needed it. Her two girls had started at the local school and Kevin's money was dwindling fast.

That afternoon, she finished washing up and mopping the floor at about five-thirty, said 'See ya' to George, her boss, and walked out to the car. She threw her bag on the front seat, saw movement out of the corner of her eye and then felt her blood freeze as Kevin stepped out of the shadows wearing that crooked smile she knew so well.

'Hi, darl,' he purred. 'Gonna give your old man a lift?'

She felt as if all the breath had been squeezed out of her lungs. She couldn't speak.

'You're lookin' well. Even though you've got that dumb look on your face.' He prowled around to her side of the car in that slow, boneless way he had.

Now her blood was moving again and carrying the message, fight or flight, but she could do neither. He came up close. She could smell beer on him.

'Dumb bitch,' he said with a cold smile. 'You can't take my money and my kids and just take off.' He looked sly. 'I suppose you wonder how I found you?'

She hadn't had time to wonder. Without warning, he sank his fist into her stomach and she fell to her knees groaning.

'You bought this ute off a dodgy car dealer, darl. Mate of mine. Paul Carroll. He owes me. He even gave me the rego number of the car. Heard the kids talking about going to Queensland. You know I won't ever let my kids be stolen from me. And you really shouldna phoned Debbie. That bitch never could keep her mouth shut. Gimme the keys,' he growled with a victor's smile.

Doubled over with pain, she managed to tell him they were on the ground, where she'd dropped them. Kevin's punch had set her brain in motion. He was either going to beat her unconscious and take her and the kids back to Sydney or he was going to kill her and bury her in the bush and take the kids back to Sydney without her. He'd often told her about people he was supposed to have killed. Junkies who hadn't paid up. He'd always told her he'd kill her if she ever left him. Overdoses. His speciality.

George looked up as the green Holden drove past the front of the coffee shop. It was Venice's car but some guy was at the wheel. George picked up the phone and dialled. He watched the car drive down the main street.

Slumped on the front seat, Venice cradled her throbbing stomach, invisible to George.

'Hello. Jenkins? Listen, mate, I think I just saw my waitress's car being stolen. Yeah, that's right. It's a green ute. It's a Holden. Heading out of town on the road past the school.' George put the phone down and went to the door. The car was long gone.

Constable Jenkins sprinted down the steps. At the bottom he met Mrs Donnelly, Clarry's sister. She was red-faced, out of breath and very agitated.

'It's Clarry. Pension day. He's gone mad again,' she rattled out like a typewriter.

Old Gittens the magistrate hadn't even handed down a custodial sentence for Clarry's last rampage.

'I've had a car reported stolen. I can't do two things at once,' Jenkins told her, pulling his cap on and sliding into the police car.

'He's on his way into town,' Mrs Donnelly tapped out. 'In the ute.'

'Silly old bugger.' Jenkins angrily slammed the car door and sped off.

Soon he saw the stolen green ute on the road out of town. Then his head whipped to the left and he saw the unmistakable, wobbling progress of Clarry's elderly blue ute approaching from the opposite direction. Jenkins had to make a decision and he took off after Clarry. A bit further on, the ute spun off the road and rolled into a paddock.

Jenkins pulled Clarry out of the ute and Clarry pulled his shiny new rifle out with him.

'Leave me alone, you bastard!' he screeched.

Jenkins tried to restrain him but he made a wild swing with the rifle which connected with Jenkins's jaw and knocked him out. Clutching the rifle, Clarry jumped in the police car and took off towards town, lights flashing.

Kevin stood in the lounge room of Venice's rented house just outside of Peppertree. 'They're not here. Where are they?' Kevin breathed beer at her and brought his fist up near her face.

She looked at her feet but then she remembered that dropping your head was a sign of submission and pulled her eyes up to meet his. 'It's a school day. I wouldn't leave them here on their own,' she said.

'You made me drive out here for nothing!' he shouted.

'You didn't say you wanted to see them.'

'Where are they?' His eyes were flashing. His mouth was a tight straight line.

When she didn't answer, he grabbed her by the arms and squeezed.

One of his favourite tortures. It hurt like hell and got results with a minimum of effort. It left marks too and he liked that. The stamp of his authority on her body.

Anger went through her like electricity and she stood on his foot as hard as she could, grinding the heel of her boot into his instep. He looked startled, then he hit her so hard that she flew backwards and hit a wall. She blacked out.

Her eyes opened and pain shot through her body, head to toe. She was in the car and Kevin was at the wheel. Through the window of the car she caught sight of a farmhouse set back from the road among some pepperina trees. The sight of it suddenly brought tears to her eyes. The farmhouse was the life she hadn't lived, or so it seemed to her. Security and respectability. An ordinary life. Something she'd once thought of as boring and stifling. She could see the man at the wheel in the pinkish light of dusk. He didn't look exciting. He looked dangerous and used up. For the first time, she could see him as he really was. A cold, ruthless, frightened man. A man who would take her life if she let him. She closed her eyes to hide the tears. He hated women crying. It made him angry.

His hand shot out and shook her. 'Wake up! Your friend phoned. Told me where to pick the kids up.' He gave a contemptuous snort.

The stupidity of women was one of the few things he believed in. He had good reason. She could see that now.

'She wondered why you hadn't picked them up. Well, you had your reasons, eh, blondie?' he drawled. He had a country and western voice for when he was especially pleased with himself. An accent as broad as the great outdoors. It was the accent he always used when he was beating her. 'Fix yourself up. You're a mess,' he told her.

He looked at her and she saw that his eyes were glassy. She thought he'd probably had a hit of speed. He looked a wreck. She dragged her bag up off the floor and brushed at her hair but stopped because it made her scalp throb as if she'd been hit with a hammer. The thought made her shiver.

He stopped the car in front of the Kelly's house and said, 'Don't say anything to her. If you do, I'll take the kids and you'll never see them again.'

Venice walked up the path on shaking legs. On either side of the path there were neat garden beds full of poppies, lupins, snapdragons and lavender. Maree Kelly loved her garden.

The door opened and Maree stood there looking worried. 'Venice, love! What happened? I was so worried and then your friend phoned. Is everything all right?' She had a frown between tiny, plucked ginger eyebrows.

Venice saw her own face in a mirror on the wall behind Maree. She looked terrible. Pale and unfocused.

'I had a migraine. I couldn't come before. Sorry.'

'Oh God, aren't they awful things? OK now, are you?'

She wanted to say, No, the darkness follows me around. I'm never OK, but she forced a smile and asked where the kids were.

Venice hurried down the path with the children following. They were arguing because they'd been watching a video and hadn't wanted to go home. When they saw Kevin, they stopped talking and stared.

Only Toby smiled. He said, 'Daddy.'

They drove in silence.

'Where are we going?' Venice finally asked him.

He just looked at her with glassy eyes and didn't answer.

Jenkins was hitchhiking. It was illegal but it was the only way he'd ever get into town. A priest on his way to a conference in Sydney stopped and Jenkins threw himself into the car.

'My car's been stolen. I have to get into Peppertree,' he told the priest.

The priest raised his eyebrows and tried not to smile. 'I'm going through Peppertree. You're in luck.'

A few minutes later, Jenkins saw the green Holden coming up fast behind the priest's car. He saw the waitress and her three children in a car with a man he didn't recognise. What the hell was going on? The Holden overtook them and continued at fantastic and unlawful speed towards Peppertree. One of the children, he thought it was a boy, looked back at them from the rear window. He saw a white face and a pink tongue which the child was poking out at them.

'Bloody hell,' Jenkins muttered in frustration and the priest raised his eyebrows again.

Soon the green Holden was just a cloud of dust on the horizon. A ghost car racing under the moon.

'I'm in a hurry,' Jenkins told the priest but he only smiled and said, 'You don't want me to speed, do you?'

Jenkins had to say no. He parted company with the priest at a service station and walked up the main street. He found Clarry lying near Blocksedge's grocery store holding his rifle. He'd passed out. The police car was parked sideways in an angle park. It wasn't damaged. Jenkins dragged Clarry over to the police car and handcuffed him to the bumper bar. He put the shiny new rifle in the boot.

Bill Blocksedge suddenly appeared. 'Listen,' he said. 'I've been talking to George and he said that waitress had left the father of her kids because he was violent. I just saw some bloke dragging her and her kids into the church. I didn't like the look of him.' Blocksedge shook his head.

Jenkins looked around and saw the green Holden on the other side of the street.

'Clarry fired at the car. I don't know if he hit anyone or not,' Blocksedge said.

'Do me a favour, Bill. Stay here and don't let anyone touch anything.'

He nodded. 'I'll do that.'

The church was lit up in preparation for the first communion classes due to be held at seven-thirty. Jenkins looked at his watch. Seven.

'Don't let him be armed,' he found himself praying. 'Dear God, don't let him be armed.'

He looked in through the shattered windscreen of the green Holden and saw some blood on the front seat. He took his gun out.

Venice put her head up and looked out one of the stained-glass windows. The window portrayed Saint Agnes being martyred. She had died horribly and Venice had no intention of following her example. The wound in her shoulder had stopped bleeding but the pain was searing. She was frightened it might make her black out. She was frightened of what might happen to her children if she did.

'Get your head down, you stupid bitch!' Kevin whispered. 'That maniac's still out there.'

He pulled her back down, sending waves of pain and nausea through her. Her head buzzed. The prelude to fainting. She took a deep breath.

'Mummy, you're not going to die, are you?' Toby was crying.

'Shut up!' Kevin took his hand back and Toby cringed, bit his lip, swallowed his tears. Merry and Talitha knew better than to say anything, but their white faces were shocking above the bright yellow shirts of their school uniforms. Venice had seen the young copper with his gun drawn sneaking up on the church. Soon it would be over. One way or another. Kevin was unarmed. He'd left his flick knife in the glovebox of the car.

Constable Jenkins rushed into the church, gun in hand, and the three children started crying, which unnerved him but didn't stop his forward motion.

Kevin didn't hesitate. He grabbed Venice and held her in front of him. 'I'm leaving and I'm taking her with me so you can't shoot me,' he shouted at Jenkins.

Venice could feel him shaking. He was a coward and yet she'd always been afraid of him. Still was.

Jenkins stood in front of the statue of the Madonna, edging up near the altar to let Kevin back past with his hostage.

The children's wails were hideous, gut-wrenching. Jenkins noticed a nerve twitching in the man's jaw as he edged by. Then he saw the waitress sink her teeth into the arm the man had around her neck. The man swore and pushed her away, lost his balance and fell at Jenkins's feet, twisting around and grabbing him by the legs. Jenkins went down and the two men struggled, crashing against the small altar where the Madonna stood, impassive and tearless. Kevin fell to the ground. The statue began to rock, then it fell on Kevin's head, knocking him out and smashing its own virtuous head to bits on the marble steps of the altar.

A few years later, Kevin would be stabbed to death in jail. He always annoyed people, sooner or later.

Venice turned away and vomited on the red carpet strip that ran along the front of the altar. Wiping her mouth on the back of her hand, she saw Father Johnson standing in the sacristy door. He raised his hands helplessly. He started telling the policeman that he'd only got the security guards out of St Michael's the week before. The Catholic Church had had to threaten legal action.

'Is the boy a Catholic, do you know?' he asked.

'He's dead, Father,' Jenkins said. 'Does it matter?'

The priest said something about God's will. Then he knelt beside the body and prayed.

Spring has covered every plant with leaves and blossoms. Haze drifts across the ocean each morning and sometimes a shower beats on the ocean and washes blossoms down on to the front path. Venice lives in a seaside town in Queensland now. Her children are brown, vigorous and settled. She is ordinary and so is her life. Most nights she sleeps but there are always those nights when she wakes and sits up in bed and watches the shadow of a tree or shrub moving on the wall. Those nights it takes a long time for her to remember that she doesn't have to be afraid any more. She is going to classes so she can matriculate. Some mornings she gazes at the haze over the ocean and dreams. Without Kevin, the possibilities seem endless.

Father Johnson puts on the rich purple vestments appropriate to the Lenten season and from where he's standing he can see the new statue of the Madonna. This one doesn't weep. Father Johnson whistles as he dresses.

Twenty Weeks in a Strange Town

We hovered over Gatton like aliens. You couldn't really say we lived there. It took a long time to be accepted in Gatton. It was a funny place. A town with an inferiority complex so virulent it should surely have produced generations of self-mutilators. The residents, however, were tough, tanned peopled with German surnames and no noticeable bits missing or cut. We spent five months there. Twenty weeks. My father managed a dairy farm for a man named George Tallis and we managed to stay alive, though the drought lasted as long as we did. Longer.

I remember driving down the range from Toowoomba in the gathering dusk. The car was overloaded and my mother was as nervous as a cat. We could feel it coming off her as we began our descent. We moved into the farmhouse at night by the light of a kerosene lamp because the generator wasn't going. Sitting in the car, we watched the light passing from room to room in the darkened farmhouse as our parents took stock of their situation. Around the car, endless blackness and endless silence made the car seem like a spaceship passing through the infinity of outer space on its way to some distant star. There were no stars to be seen, though, the night we moved in.

The silence got to my mother in the end. She hadn't been able to bring her beloved piano. We didn't even have a radio. Basically, I think she had some kind of nervous breakdown. Her problem was that she 'thought herself', in the term commonly used in those days to cut tall poppies down to size. Being a farmer's wife on this little farm, blasted by heat and drought by day and swamped by silence and darkness at night was not how she had imagined her life. She was a trained singer with a beautiful lyric soprano voice who had been offered a contract with the BBC in London; but her eyes had met my father's over a bucket of milk on another dairy farm where he was working at the time. My father had beautiful brown eyes and looked a lot like Rudolf Valentino and my mother's beautiful blue eyes had been blinded by infatuation, or so it seemed she had come to believe.

She was too good for this farm wife existence and, after alternating between resentment and profound depression for the first month, she developed insomnia and anxiety. Six kids to care for, including an energetic toddler, and a husband who was as happy as a pig in mud. She felt as if she was losing her mind. Some nights she would make us all kneel in the lounge room and say the rosary over and over until the storm in her mind had passed. Eyes closed, the black jet of the rosary beads glinting as they passed through her fingers, she prayed for deliverance. She called on every Catholic saint and the Holy Trinity – Father, Son and Holy Ghost. My father didn't stand a chance.

We children found our feelings were divided. We loved the farm and hated Gatton and every simple, twisted soul in the place. The kids at the convent school we went to had read about martyrs and when they saw us they decided that's what we were. We were poor and oh so numerous and cursed with the kind of flashy good looks that meant our tatty second-hand uniforms and the tangled hair that our distracted mother only sometimes got around to brushing could never go unnoticed. We were made to feel dirty and stupid. If they had to associate with us, they did it by making faces and insulting us. Some days, I hoped our mother's prayers were working but twenty weeks is a lifetime to a child so after a while we all assumed this hell was our lot and a punishment for some sin or other.

The life we had left behind in Toowoomba looked better all the time. We didn't even have a radio. We could remember gardens that weren't drought-blasted and street lights and the corner shop and the milkman. We remembered our bit of civilisation as if we were exiles remembering a golden age that would never come again. We travelled around the district and into Gatton in a black FJ Holden that had a drunk's thirst for petrol and it was a long way from the farm to the school. One day with my mother at the wheel the car ran out of petrol on the dirt road that led to the farm. We looked at the tinder-dry bush around us, stared up the sandy, yellowish road that seemed to lead nowhere and then up at the vast, pitiless blue sky that didn't seem to know how to rain. We were alone, far from all assistance. My mother tried to look calm but we could all see the state she was in. Her eyes darted here, there and everywhere.

'If only Dad would come,' said the youngest in a small voice and a flicker of hope seemed to cross my mother's face. Of course. When we didn't arrive home he would come looking for us.

Time passed. How much time it was impossible to say. No one had a watch.

Then over a distant hill came a lone horsemen. It was our father on Dolly, the brown mare, with a petrol can strapped to her saddle. We laughed and clapped our hands but our mother just stared straight ahead. Her mouth was beginning to be tugged down on one side with resignation and despair. The days in the sun had darkened the freckles she hated until they stood out as if they'd been pencilled on. Deliverance had better come soon. My father filled the car with petrol and Mum drove home in silence with that same calm, defeated look. The one that made her look like a stranger.

The months passed but the seasons never really seemed to change. It was hot and dry or hot and windy or stiflingly hot and dry. The cows paraded in and out of the dairy regular as clockwork and the big silver cans of milk and cream were picked up and taken away. We were all burnt darkest brown by the sun and ran wild around the farm when we weren't being martyred at school. Then there were times when our mother would get that dutiful look on her face and take us off to the Gatton library: an oasis of cool and peace for our tortured mother and a feast of reading for us. Television was yet to come so we spent lots of nights curled up with books that seemed to open an escape hatch. Those were times when we truly hovered over Gatton, astral travellers floating on a silver thread in the black immensity of the night sky until our eyelids closed like curtains on the pages.

Crisis point for my mother was finally reached when we woke one day to find that Dolly had pushed the car into the dam, bonnet first.

'She must've scratched her rump on it,' my father said, unfazed by this disaster.

My mother said nothing. Just walked away. We danced around like little Indians, whooping for joy. We couldn't go to school. It seemed like a miracle. We went into the house to finish our breakfast but as we sat at the table a terrible sound, something like an animal in pain, echoed through the farmhouse. It was our mother crying in the bedroom up the hall. We all fell silent and my father's face took on a sad and perplexed expression. He left the table and walked up the hall. The crying didn't stop and then we heard him go out the front door and slam it. I suddenly felt we were all poised on the edge of some kind of disaster. I was only eleven but I was the eldest and I had been taught to take my position as eldest seriously. It was a position of responsibility and trust and I knew my mother was at breaking point.

By lunchtime, a truck passing through the property had pulled the car out of the dam and my father had got it going. My mother had stopped crying by then but we knew better than to venture up the hall before we left for school.

Some weeks went by and then one day as my father sat having what he called his smoko, George Tallis appeared at the front door. My father walked up the hall smiling, all hail-fellow-well-met, but after talking to Tallis he came back unsmiling and very white in the face. I thought someone had died. He sat down, though, and finished eating his food. He calmly sipped his tea but his face was whiter than ever. Then he went up the hall and we heard him talking to our mother. She spent a lot of time just lying in the bedroom now. His low angry voice and hers, high and startled, sang a kind of duet.

From the snippets we overheard, we realised that we would be leaving the farm, leaving Dolly, leaving our wild, dry Wonderland. We ate in silence for a while until the realisation that we would be leaving our martyrdom too made us all start talking again. The drought had bitten too deep. Tallis was selling the farm. Our mother's prayers had ambushed our father at last.

When we left, I took a lot of memories with me but the one I will never forget is my mother's face as the overloaded car rumbled down the sandy track away from the farmhouse. She turned and looked back at the house like a woman who had survived a life-threatening illness: her face pale and otherworldly. She seemed to me to be wounded in a way that would take a long time to heal.

'Good thing we didn't sell the house in Toowoomba,' my father said.

I watched her turn away and look out the window of the car at the dry, half-dead trees we were passing. Bark hung off them in strips.

'You wanted to sell it,' I heard my mother say. 'You would have if I hadn't stopped you.'

I don't think she ever really trusted him again.

Europe on the Yarra

It had been a desperate year, though desperation is always relative. My father died in January and even though it was my mother who dominated our affections and our lives, after my father died the family began to implode. Having lost the status quo, we began in subtle ways to lose ourselves.

I was unaware of this when I boarded a plane to Melbourne with my brother. My first sight of Melbourne filled me with foreboding. I had never been there before. It was raining when we got off the plane and my brother had made no plans for us to be picked up by someone named Greg. That is, he had made no useful plans.

'How will he know us?'

'He's driving a maroon station wagon.'

'But how will he know us? Have you ever met him?'

'No.'

'Do you know his mobile number?'

This he knew. I phoned the number but it went to voicemail. I left a message, a strange, disjointed one but one which told Greg we were waiting near the taxi rank at the airport.

At some point, I got agitated and raised my voice. 'I can't believe you didn't make arrangements,' I whined. 'Do you realise how many maroon station wagons there could be around this airport?'

Petulant as a small child, he flounced off to the car park. The car park! He was looking for a man he had never seen and therefore couldn't recognise in an enormous car park full of… Had he always been this strange? This unreasonable? I watched him wandering the car park like a lost soul and realised for the first time that that was exactly what he was. My agitation increased as the minutes passed and the cars circled the

airport and the taxis came and went. My brother strode the car park like a
prophet with a vision of the world that no one else could see.

Then the maroon station wagon was there with Greg at the wheel. I
assumed it was Greg by the way he was staring curiously at the people on
the taxi rank. I waved and he sprang out and took my suitcase.

'Hello. I'm Greg.'

My brother had returned from the car park.

'I left my mobile at home,' said Greg with a tight smile. 'I came to the
airport and drove around for about fifteen minutes then I went back to
get the mobile and got your message.'

I considered him for a while and decided he was not to be relied on.
This knowledge gave me a warped kind of pleasure: the nihilistic pleasure
of disconnection. I already knew the holiday would be a disaster and it
hadn't even begun. I started to panic but there was no turning back and no
going back until Sunday. We had bought bargain basement airline tickets
which meant we had to stay in Melbourne until Sunday or pay more. I
had no more and I refused to run away in any case but the knowledge that
there was no escape didn't help. It accelerated my panic but I got in the
station wagon and pretended all was well.

Melbourne was so foreign to me it might as well have been part of
another country. It wasn't like Brisbane. Or Sydney. Or London. Or Paris.
Or Rome. I couldn't relate it to anything else. For one thing, it was spring
and Melbourne was freezing and rainy. Like Europe but not Europe. Only
later did I come to understand that the alienation was in me. Incurable and
insistent. A pathology. In some strange way, Melbourne was a reflection of
my innermost strangeness and isolation. I recoiled from it in horror but
it was myself I feared.

To the house in Brunswick. Greg's partner (I can't remember her name
but she should have had a name like Tiffany) wasn't there. She was a music
teacher and she was out – teaching music. There were dogs – Harold and
Mick – and there was dog fur and dust and squalor and one beautiful
room. It was all beige and blond pine and eerily tidy with a TV, stereo and
well-stocked bookcases. It was who they really were. The rest of the house

with its bohemian chaos was who they wanted to be. This room became my haven. It reminded me that I had rooms like it back in Queensland. A home. A place I belonged. I started to think like a soldier. This was something that had to be endured: like battle.

That afternoon we went to Fitzroy and suddenly the world closed in on me and I thought I would crack up. You'll be in a psych ward. You'll be left in this place and he'll go home. Back to the sun. Back to our imploding family. Breakdown. I had been there. In Fitzroy, I could have gone there again. The history of the place was ingrained in every brick. Those cramped two-storey buildings with the roofs that extended over the pavement and rested on two posts. A western town with no sheriff and no horses, it stretched as far as the eye could see in either direction. So familiar and so strange that I went through another life as I stared at it. Poor, working class, often cold, always hungry and always stuck in Fitzroy. Carried out in a coffin. I died and it was the nineteenth century and then I flew back into my body and it was the twenty-first. I was in my own little hell.

'Let's find a place to eat. It's cheap here,' my brother said.

It had always been cheap in Fitzroy. It was a place where people had always made do and had to struggle for the necessities of life.

'Okay,' I said. 'I'm hungry too.'

That wasn't true but I thought I was less likely to fall apart if I ate something. We had huge, steaming bowls of seafood pasta in a barn of a place: kitschy, arty and cavernous. The pasta was five dollars a pop and I ate as if it could cure me of what ailed me. It didn't.

'You have to see Carlton,' my brother said.

What was Carlton to me? My brother had lived in Melbourne for a year and he knew where you were supposed to go. The monuments: Weary Dunlop and Blamey. The painting of Chloe up the stairs in a restaurant. Out of breath, I gazed on Chloe while my brother worried that a waiter would approach and we might have to buy a drink or, worse still, a meal.

We ran down the stairs and he was saying, 'There's a double on at the Astor. I checked. *Tais-toi* and *The Closet*.'

I had already seen *The Closet* but my brother said we would have to watch both once we had paid. Feeling trapped, knowing that I had already done too much and needed an early night, I agreed. I would regret it and I knew I would regret it but by now I was so sick with nerves that I was afraid to be afraid. Afraid to take precautions or to forestall suffering. I thought that one moment of hesitation was all that was needed to make me lose my grip.

Adding to the impression of being lost in the nineteenth century was the presence of beggars, seemingly on every street corner. Some just openly begged, others had sheets of poems to shield themselves from the fact that they were beggars. Was this Australia? It couldn't be, could it? Was this the twenty-first century?

At the Astor, I took in the beauty – the carpets, the stairs and the chandelier – and ate a mango ice cream. I thanked God for Gerard Depardieu and *Tais-toi*. He made me laugh. *The Closet* made me laugh too, even though I had seen it before.

Afterwards we ran up Bourke Street to catch a tram. It was close to midnight. I didn't tell my brother that the reason we couldn't catch the train was that the whooshing rush of the trains fanned my panic and agitation to fever pitch. He didn't argue about catching the tram. By then the strain was clearly visible on my face. My suffering was now felt as a tingling sensation that seemed to affect every nerve and every cell in my body. Jumping out of my skin. I personified the saying as the tram clattered along all thirty-six stops to Brunswick.

It was around one a.m. when I got to bed in the outside shed, converted into a flat, where I was to stay. I couldn't get warm, couldn't calm down and had no sleep until I stumbled through the dark across the yard and into the beautiful room, where I slept on the beige carpet for a couple of hours.

The next day I met Tiffany (why can't I remember her name? Is it Freudian?) I gave her and Greg a gift: copies of my two existing books. A collection of essays and volume one of an autobiography. It was a mistake. They were creative people themselves, so I had thought. A musician/music lecturer and a music teacher/musician. But they looked at the books in bewilderment and studied me furtively as if I had two heads and they were trying not to notice. I knew from his face that Greg had already picked up on my vibe of repressed hysteria so I thought that for him the books could be some kind of an explanation for my jumpy and distracted manner. For Tiffany, they probably represented a threat. Either way, it was a mistake. It cut me off yet again when I needed a link and a lifeline. I had simply thought I was being thrifty not buying them gifts.

Greg had brown hair and brown eyes. He was solid, even-tempered. Tiffany was a slender, long-limbed blonde. My brother lusted after her but now there was Greg and the dogs and this quasi domesticity. They were a version of the eternal triangle and that isolated me even more.

I experienced everything around me intensely but I was also locked in silent battle with the strange feelings that inhabited me along with the acceptable me: wife, mother, sister, writer, productive member of society. The fear was that one day those feelings would take over and the acceptable me would disappear. I knew from my research into my malady that everyone who suffered as I did had the same fear. What if. These things are private and shameful. They couldn't be discussed except with those who had the same affliction. A secret society of suffering. At some point we took a tram to St Kilda. The palm trees reminded me of Queensland but they were all wrong. Growing out of the pavements like props in a play. We went to a café and had tiramisu.

'The only authentic tiramisu. The others are not made to the authentic recipe,' my brother told me.

He took photos of me and of the palm trees and the art installations on some of the buildings. I smiled. I laughed. I wanted to go home.

We went to the Shrine of Remembrance. I was thinking that going into this place would be impossible for me but there was such an atmosphere of peace that I went down the steps and into this temple of death with only the slightest flutter of dread. The tour guide told us ecstatically about the shaft of light that came through a special opening at a certain time of the year and lit up words inscribed on a plaque. Thoughts crowded into my head. Her words made me think about Stonehenge, human sacrifice, the Aztecs. I stared at the walls and saw that they were covered in the names of the dead.

'It's like an Egyptian tomb, isn't it?' my brother asked her.

'Oh yes,' she said. 'It was influenced by Egyptian architecture.'

And Greek. And Roman. All pagans. The hero cult. The cult of death. And the survivors? The legless, the armless, the witless, the beggars. They were not depicted. Their names were not here because they weren't dead. This mausoleum was not about them. I looked up to the ceiling, high above us. It really was a beautiful building. Something hovered on the edges of my mind. Hitler. Hitler and his buildings. Fascism. The word sidled up to me. Shyly, like a child edging onstage. This is what the pacifists were up against. I pictured them being crushed by the weight of this building: by its mythology, by its statues, its shaft of light which illuminated not the darkness but words picked out in gold on a plaque. I bought a pencil sharpener in the shape of a cannon. The pencil went in under the barrel. Out on the balcony of the Shrine of Remembrance, we surveyed Melbourne from on high. The green of the trams running at the bottom of the hill gave me motion sickness. And vertigo.

'Let's go in,' I said. 'Let's go and have coffee.'

This building had been made for those whose hearts had been torn out and weighed against a feather. My father had survived World War Two and gone into Nagasaki with the occupation forces. He hadn't suffered from bad nerves. His sunny disposition was legendary in our family.

On our last day in Melbourne, we went to Heide to see the paintings and to experience the John and Sunday Reed legend. My brother claimed admission was free and when we discovered it wasn't he and Tiffany went off to walk around the gardens and left me to myself. I glided ghostlike around the rooms of Heide. There seemed to be no one else around. Here was order, furniture polish and money.

Then I stopped, riveted, in front of Danila Vassilief's *Valerie and Betty*. Fitzroy again. Two working-class girls standing in the foreground with those double-storey working-class buildings behind them. I studied the muddy browns and drab greens of the girls' dresses and the tin-grey sky of the painting before moving on.

For some reason (the gods are so capricious), in the library at Heide I had the first moments of peace I had experienced since arriving in Melbourne. I wanted to touch the ruby-red covers of some of the books but they were behind glass. The pale sun came into the room through the window and shone on my silence and my newborn serenity. We were leaving in the morning. Perhaps it was that. Whatever it was, when I stood before Moya Dyring's portrait of Sunday Reed, the cool, pastel colours seemed to touch my skin and I felt my fever breaking. Inexplicably, my mood shifted and the panic and fear left me exactly as they had arrived – out of the blue.

On the plane out of Melbourne, I was calm. I ate anaemic pasta with a plastic spoon and sipped juice. We were flying in the dark and I hadn't seen the earth receding. That was a plus.

At Brisbane airport, my husband was waiting near the baggage carousel. He knew how to collect travellers. He knew where to wait. He always had a plan. Always read the instructions when he bought a blender. Always filled in the warranty. I had never appreciated him more. In the car my sister-in-law's dog was waiting. I didn't like the dog all that much but I was glad to see it. It was part of life's normal irritations. We were always looking after her dog for one reason or another and I normally resented it. I found I didn't resent it.

We dropped my brother at his house and set off for home. I closed my eyes and saw the Vassilief painting. What did it mean, the way I had felt in Fitzroy? Perhaps Vassilief had put those houses in a painting because they disturbed him the way Fitzroy had disturbed me. Perhaps that was what art was for. Was this an epiphany? Flying along in the dark beside my husband I understood for the first time why I had really married him and was amazed at how wise I had been at twenty-one. Or how prescient. I watched the white headlights picking out the road ahead. Exhausted, yet philosophical, I quoted Robert Frost to myself: 'For once, then, something.'

To Breathe

London 1822

'So,' Doctor Benson said, 'do you see these angels in the trees all the time or only sometimes?'

The old man he'd spoken to was not an inmate of Benson's asylum. Benson was compiling a case history on him, though, for the archive of his mental hospital. Through their mutual friend, Mr Robinson, Benson had offered the impoverished old man a guinea to be interviewed. He regarded the old man as a most interesting case.

The old man looked at Benson kindly. It was almost a look of pity and the thought came to Benson that the poor fellow actually felt sorry for him. An intolerable thought or at the very least a discomfiting one.

'I see angels when they're there,' the old man said, reasonably.

His white hair stood out around his head and shafts of light from the window illuminated it so that he seemed to have a halo himself. There was in any case something luminous and strange about the fellow. His clothes were worn but not worn-out and his large brown eyes were shrewd and full of life. What was it about him that made him seem so odd? Dammed if he could put his finger on it, but the mad always looked strange. Whether it was because they knew they were mad or suspected others knew, he couldn't say. All his years of experience had never answered that question – and many others.

'Are you a spiritual man?' Doctor Benson asked.

The old man smiled and looked out the window. He seemed not have heard.

'The word spiritual comes from the Latin *spirare*, to breathe,' he said.

'We cannot avoid breathing, can we? Spirituality is our natural state. How then can I avoid it?'

Those extraordinary eyes. The fellow had done those violent and blasphemous paintings. They were like nothing Benson had ever seen before, full of nude bodies and strange colours, but were they the work of a genius or a madman? As soon as he saw those paintings, he wanted to meet the man who'd painted them. Especially when he heard from others that he was regarded as a mad genius. Madness and genius were closely allied, he knew that; but could anyone be both? The thought came unbidden that society could not and would not permit anyone to be both. It was too disruptive of the idea of an orderly society. The genius was a sort of hero and a hero could not be mad.

'Your paintings are very unusual. Very striking indeed. How do you paint them?'

'Well,' the old man was looking out the window again, 'I take a millboard, thick is best for my purpose. Then I take ink or colour and I make a design very quickly so that no colour has time to dry. This I print on to paper and then I colour it up in watercolour.' He looked at Benson and his eyes were gleaming. He gestured excitedly as he spoke. 'The advantage of this method, for my purpose at least, is that each print can be varied slightly so that no two are the same. That's the way it is with human beings, is it not?'

'No two the same?'

He smiled and now his eyes gleamed with mischief. Benson felt uncomfortable and off balance somehow.

'And your themes? Are they always biblical?'

'There is much to learn in the Bible and much to unlearn.' The old man's eyes were now focused on something, perhaps some scene from the Old Testament, just to the right of Benson's head.

'Do the angels tell you what to paint?'

'Not that I'm aware of. I've never spoken to them or attempted to communicate with them in any way.'

'Why not?'

'Because, my dear sir, it's enough for me that they exist. I ask nothing more of them,' he laughed softly and looked straight at Benson.

The doctor flinched and looked away. Who could bear the scrutiny of eyes that saw angels? Benson had to check himself at this point. Thinks he sees angels, he told himself firmly. Delusional. He reached for the word and held on to it. The old fellow's face had an expression of exceptional sweetness when it was not animated by some strong emotion.

'Are you happy with your life?' Benson asked him.

'I live for art, as I always have. I wanted no other trade and I have had no other. Yes, I'm happy. Though it is a happiness few understand. You yourself would find it as impossible to understand my happiness as the camel would find it to pass through the eye of the needle. I don't hold it against you, though, nor should you hold my strange happiness against me.'

The old man was thinking as he spoke that to tell this doctor, this imprisoner of the mad, that he spoke regularly with a being he thought of as 'the Spirit' or that he was assailed constantly by visions which the doctor would see as hallucinations would be most unwise. He would not be unwise.

'You write poetry too, I've heard.'

'Yes.'

'Can I hear a poem?'

The old man immediately spoke in a clear, pleasant voice. 'When he hath tried me, I shall come forth like gold. Have pity on me, O ye my friends, for the hand of God hath touched me.'

'But surely that's…'

'From the Bible. Yes, it is. You asked to hear a poem and that's what the Old Testament is.' The man sniffed and looked away.

While Doctor Benson remained convinced that the old man was mad, he felt as if he (the sane one, the physician) was floundering and being tested somehow.

'What are you working on at the moment?'

'An engraving of Dante's *Inferno*. My poems are mostly very long,' he said as if apologising for his former behaviour. 'And difficult,' he added. 'I'll be using some of the guinea you're paying me, in the making of my engraving, I expect.'

Benson felt pleased and despised himself for it. 'You realise you'll probably die poor, don't you?' he told the old man by way of revenge, though he wouldn't have called it that. He would have called it research.

'I'll die and I'll certainly be poor when I do it but the imagination lives forever and art and money are bad bedfellows. Do you know of Thomas Lawrence?'

'I don't, no.'

'Nor will you. He's a rich man, like you. A fashionable portrait painter. His name will die with him. Mine will not die with me. One day the world will know my achievements for what they are. You know, Mr Thomas gave me twenty pounds because he felt sorry for me, but,' he leaned forward, eyes bright, 'I feel far sorrier for him. Poor fellow.' He shook his head.

Benson thought that one of the advantages of being mad was that one's delusions gave certainty – something no amount of rational thought could give. The old man had faith. He believed that even his poverty was a sign of his future greatness.

'So, you're laying up riches in heaven.' Benson couldn't keep the smirk out of his voice, though he managed to keep it off his face.

'Not at all. I'm simply doing what I was meant to do with my life. I agree with you in one respect – I was not meant for this world. Indeed not. This world and I are not friends; I've known that since I was a child. I saw my first angels when I was a child of eight. They filled an entire tree and they shone like stars. Their wings were so bright they blinded me. It was some time before I could see again and when I could the angels had gone. I sat down on the ground and wept. I wanted them to come back. I'm sure the memory of their beauty is what led me to art.'

'You were obviously a child of powerful imagination.' Benson spoke smoothly and calmly and the old man turned to him with that sweet expression.

'Of course I was. But I didn't imagine it. No, not at all.' His face was closed now. His mouth stubborn.

Benson decided he'd gone too far. The last thing he wanted was a distressing scene or even a collapse that would necessitate admitting the old man to the asylum. He was not someone that Benson wanted to have to see or know about while he went about his business with his lunatics. The man was not only disturbed, he was disturbing. Or at least Benson found him so. He had dealt with all kinds of lunatics – cursing, spinning, raving, violent and catatonic – but he had never been as disturbed by them as he was by this man.

But now it was suddenly obvious to Benson why this old man saw angels. When one thought about his life, it was easy to understand. Here was a man who craved the beautiful and the sacred, and how did he live? Surrounded by the ugliness of the modern city and the sordidness of its inhabitants; constantly assailed in ear and eye and even in thought by the profane. The life of the impoverished artist could be a long suicide – it could lead to despair – yet this man seemed happy and fulfilled. Dissatisfied with the world he lived in, he had created another world of angels, sacred deeds, great sin and a hope of redemption that many of the poor who lived on London's streets and in its hovels had lost. His world was one of delusion but it had saved him from despair and defeat. He had re-created the world. He was his own Messiah. The dangers in this were obvious to Benson, though he had to admit there were no signs of 'delusions of grandeur' in this man. He was humble and sweet-natured.

In a last attempt to stamp his authority on the proceedings, Benson asked him, 'Where did you train as an artist?'

'When I was ten, my parents sent me to Henry Par's Drawing School which is at 101 The Strand. It's on the right-hand side as you go into the city, as you probably know.'

Benson didn't and began to feel that there were probably a large number of things this old man knew that he didn't. He twisted away from the feeling.

'Even Michelangelo,' the man went on, 'once remarked that it was necessary to learn to draw correctly in youth. Many people have told me I'm an exceptional draughtsman. I was taught at the right age, you see.'

Benson nodded. 'Were your parents religious?' he asked him.

'My parents were dissenters and they espoused radical politics. Don't seek an answer there to the course my life has taken. Shakespeare has one of his characters say that a man is author of himself and knows no other kin. That is certainly the case with myself. My mother even beat me once for speaking of my visions.' The sweet expression slipped briefly and bitterness took its place. 'Only once, but I never forgot it.'

Soon after, Benson terminated the interview and paid the old man his guinea.

'Thank you, sir. It's been most interesting,' the old fellow said, as if Benson had been the subject of his research and not he of Benson's. Then with a slight bow he went on his way.

As the strange old man was walking away, Doctor Friars came out of the adjoining room. The connecting door had been left slightly ajar so that Friars could take notes for his own research purposes. Friars had a chilling presence (which was most unfortunate since he had a first-class mind) and he often had an unsettling effect on the patients. When he swept down the halls of the asylum in the long black cloak he favoured, he looked like a large bat. The lunatics had been known to fall to their knees and address him as 'God'.

Benson turned to Friars and said, 'Well, he's certainly mad but he's harmless.'

Friars did not agree and would have locked him up in an instant. Friar's eyes narrowed. 'What's his name?'

Benson told him and he wrote it neatly at the top of the file that he held in his hand. 'William Blake' he wrote in his beautiful handwriting.

Being in possession of a guinea, the old man was able to travel back to his house in Fountain Court by coach. He paid the coachman, walked up to his front door and knocked.

His wife opened it. She was very pale and looked almost ready to faint. 'Oh, my dear!' she gasped. 'I thought I'd never see you again. The thought of you in that horrible place was more than I could bear.'

Her husband helped her to a chair. 'Sit down, Catherine,' he said in a kindly way, and went to fetch her a tumbler of water.

'What did he say? The doctor? And did he pay you?'

'So many questions, my dear. Don't distress yourself. He was very pleasant and yes, he gave me a guinea. Now I can begin the engraving.'

'But what did he say?' his wife insisted.

'He said I was harmless,' he shouted, suddenly furious. He threw the tumbler of water across the room and swept their already cracked and chipped dishes off a sideboard on to the floor, where they made a satisfying smash.

His wife looked at him in surprise and then she started to laugh.

He found he had to laugh too. 'Harmless!' he laughed and shouted. He threw the word out the open window as if it was a lighted flare or a dagger.

The people in the neighbouring houses heard the shouting and laughing but they were used to strange goings-on in that house.

The angels in the tree outside his back door smiled at each other. Their man was in fine form today. Soon, they knew, he would pick up pen or brush and go on with his work. They liked to watch him work. They liked to toss ideas his way and then watch the passion they aroused at work in him. Incapable of passion themselves, they still had an appreciation of it. They knew it was what moved the planets; that the whole incredible machinery of creation had been born of it and that this man also needed it to create. He existed between two worlds, as they did. His was the mind that would have been theirs had they been matter and not spirit.

That night in bed with his wife asleep beside him, the old man remembered going down the steps of the lunatic asylum, quite happy and a guinea richer, when he became aware of something moving at one of the barred windows. He looked back and saw one of the lunatics rocking backwards and forwards, his eyes upraised and his mouth moving as if in prayer or perhaps in conversation with someone who existed only in his mind. The old man watched the rocking man behind the barred window and as he did he put into the lunatic's mouth the words he himself had written:

> Oh why was I born with a different face?
> Why was I not born like the rest of my race?

He had hurried down the steps then, afraid that he had seen a vision of his own future.

Now, lying awake in the dark, he knew that he had to think of something else or he would never sleep, so he remembered himself at the age of ten. It was high summer and he had eaten blackberries from some bushes on the edge of the road. He saw himself on that golden day, red-haired and rosy-cheeked, sturdy and joyous as he tramped along the road. Then he saw all the moments of his life as if they were beads on a string and felt for the first time that he could make sense of them. He watched his ten-year-old self sitting at the kitchen table with a piece of paper he had found in a drawer, with pen and ink. He marvelled at the innocence and, above all, the hopefulness of the boy as he started to write his poem. All the old man's faith in his past and in his destiny came back as he read the first two lines the boy had written:

> How sweet I roam'd from field to field.
> And tasted all the summer's pride.

Soon he slept. And dreamed no dreams.

Waiting for the Storm

The barbershop was still on the corner of Grey and Makim Streets in the country town where I grew up. Tom Kelleher the barber would be in his late sixties now but the sign still read 'T. Kelleher, Barber'. His hand was as steady as ever, they said.

If I drove down the main street, a million memories rose to meet me. Some of them were better not remembered.

My mother had been ill for some time before she died. Breast cancer. I had been there the night she died but my father had been out doing what he always did when he couldn't face things: getting drunk. Next morning someone found him, an old man with a hangover, lying in a heap in someone's yard with the skin gone off both his elbows.

I hadn't spoken to my father for years but when my mother knew she was dying, I came back from the city where I had made a new life to look after her. The cancer was advanced by the time they found it and they told her the outlook was grim from the start. She accepted it the way she had accepted that she loved a man who would never be there for her; a man who would abuse her viciously when he was drunk and find ways of making their marriage into a kind of martyrdom for her.

The mystery for me was that she never stopped loving him. Her saintly nature made him hate himself but it didn't make him stop drinking.

'Not even God Himself could make your father stop drinking,' she told me once (I must have been about twelve), and I can still remember the uneasy smile that followed the words. I knew she would go to the priest and confess – what? That she had judged her husband?

I learned to hate him. When I left home, I begged her to go with me. I wanted to save her the way she saved me when he went after me with the thick, brown belt that held his baggy trousers up. She had put me firmly behind her and refused to move. He raised the belt and I felt a scream rising in my throat, but he didn't hit her that time.

'You're not to touch her,' I heard my mother say in her clear, deep voice. Her hands, holding me to her back, trembled but her voice didn't.

He finally moved away, muttering and swearing; weaving drunkenly through the house.

One of the most overpowering memories from my childhood was the smell of his vomit and the smell of the Pine O Kleen she always used to disinfect the spot. There was no shifting that smell and there was no shifting his drunkenness. It lived with us. We dreamed it. Breathed it in as we slept. It owned us and so did he.

My brother Paul would be arriving soon for the funeral. It would be held at the Catholic church, Sacred Heart, which was just down the road from the low-set weatherboard house (two bedrooms, a downstairs laundry, a small veranda on the front) that had been my parent's home since they bought it as newly-weds in 1961. I had an angry conversation with Paul just before he moved out, about leaving our mother alone in that house with him.

'What can I do? She thinks he's sick and he needs her help. She thinks a wife has to see it through, to stay in sickness and health and all that shit.' He thought about it for a while. 'The trouble is,' he said, smiling our mother's smile – he took after her side of the family – 'I know his dirty little secret. He gets drunk so he can be cruel. It allows him to behave that way. She thinks it's the drink that makes him cruel. She doesn't know his secret.'

I was the one who had inherited my father's dark hair and green eyes. It scared me. Did it mean I would be a drunk too?

Once the funeral was arranged, I moved out of the weatherboard house and into Maher's boarding house three streets away.

'Are you going to leave me here on my own?' my father had piped piteously, hung over and strangely shrunken in his armchair. The one she bought him for his sixtieth birthday.

I could picture him sitting in it watching the football while my mother bought him stubbies and then carried the empty bottles away. Until he got angry. Then she would go into the bedroom and lie in bed saying the rosary. He would drink until he passed out and spend the night in the recliner chair. It meant he didn't have to fall over trying to make his way to bed.

'You'll be fine,' I said.

'You don't care if I am or not,' he whined.

'No,' I said. 'I don't.'

'You always were a cold little bitch,' he said, very cold and self-righteous himself now. 'That's why you're a writer,' he sneered. He was very pleased with himself for thinking of that.

'Paul will pick you up and take you to the funeral,' I said, ignoring his attack. 'I'm sure you'd prefer him to help you shower and dress.'

'I can shower and dress myself! What are you talking about?'

That was just the daylight talking. When night came and the wind whistled around the house, he would remember everything he'd ever done to her and he would go to the fridge and start drinking. I wasn't sure he would be in a fit state even to attend the funeral. I certainly wasn't staying the night in that house with him. The ghosts of Christmas Past would be walking there all night, strolling in their matey way back and forth from bed to fridge with my father, telling him what a great man he was. I had no intention of cleaning up and wielding the disinfectant bottle.

The day of the funeral, Paul came to Maher's boarding house before he went to see my father. To check the lie of the land. That's how it always was. Our lives when we were growing up had to be arranged around our father's drunkenness. It was a habit now.

'What's he like? How's he handling it?'

'He was fine when I left him but you know him…'

'Indeed I do. Will he be hungover, do you think?'

'Better if he is. He'll be too sick to make a scene.'

We nodded, orderlies to our father's madman. He would dominate our mother's funeral as he had dominated her life.

'His suit's been dry-cleaned. It's in the bedroom cupboard still in the plastic, so it'll be easy to find. His shoes are in the shoe rack in the laundry.

If he's sick, I left some Berocca in the bathroom cupboard. Better than nothing. Give him coffee too and make him eat something. Buy him one of those caramel milkshakes he likes. If all else fails, make sure he drinks that.'

'You've thought of everything,' Paul smiled. He looked even more like our mother now that he was older.

Being the children of such a dreadful marriage had made us tough. I was cold. My father was right about that. I had watched my mother love and nurture all of us and I saw what had happened to her. I told myself I was my father's daughter now. Then I thought about the dry-cleaned suit, the Berocca, the shoes, the milkshake. My father won by inertia because, in the final analysis, he was as irresponsible as a two-year-old. Paul drove off in his girlfriend's car. She wasn't coming. She didn't like funerals.

As I dressed to go to the funeral, I remembered something that I hadn't thought about for years. The night my brother and I had retreated to the bedroom we shared, because our drunken father was threatening and haranguing our mother in the lounge room.

'Stupid bitch!' he kept saying. 'Stupid, bloody bitch!' while our mother floundered around trying to placate him. Falling back from one position after another until she was cornered at last against the lounge room wall.

'Go to your bedroom,' she told us, white-faced.

There was a storm coming. The sky was almost black and a deathly silence had fallen. Into this silence our father's drunken, vicious insults flew like arrows. Occasionally, thunder rolled and lightning lit up the sky far away. We could smell the rain that would soon arrive and there was the sound of a bird with a call that was midway between a drumbeat and a crazed laugh adding its song to our father's ranting. It seemed a bird of ill-omen to me. We went to the window, Paul and I, and looked out. Suddenly the wind became a frantic rushing. There was a fierce drumming as the wind beat on the trees, on the roof and on the ground hurling dust around. I thought I could hear that beating sound inside our house. My father was like that wind: reckless, careless and violent. I was terribly afraid. I must have been about eight years old then and Paul would have been around five. I went over to a little desk I had near my bed and picked up the weapon that I didn't yet know was a weapon. The pen slid smoothly over the piece of paper, far more eager than I to get to work. The words were nicely formed even though I was shaking with fear – and with rage. 'I hate my father,' I wrote. 'I wish he would die.' The storm broke and the rain came crashing down. I started to cry because of what I had written. Paul joined in out of fear and we sobbed and wailed as the rain lashed the house. I remember the feeling I had – that there was no safety anywhere; inside the house or out. In a way, I suppose I've never lost that feeling.

The funeral went smoothly. I was numb. I didn't cry. My father looked terrible. He had a hangover, as I had known he would, and his face was grey above his dark blue suit as he watched the coffin descend to the strains of 'Danny Boy'. His stricken look would have been mistaken for grief by most of the mourners, especially those who had known and loved my mother. But in truth, like most addicts, my father was a monster of selfishness and she had escaped into the grave – an irreversible escape. There was a moment when he came towards me (at the wake held after the funeral in a local hall) and seemed to want to hug or kiss me. I turned my back on him and after that we revolved like two satellites – in parallel orbits but never touching. One hangover was behind him and another one would be faced tomorrow. And so it would go on.

In the early hours of the morning, I kissed Paul goodbye and drove down the main street heading out of town. Past the barber's and all the ghostly buildings from a past full of pain. My mother was in her grave now and I wondered as I turned my car on to the open road if the little girl who wrote those hate-filled words on a piece of paper would free herself from them before she died. I drove along the lonely highway, no radio, listening to the steady hum of the engine.

Later, as the sky lightened, I could hear my mother's voice, the exact, edgy tone of it, calling from the lighted house into darkness filled with the song of summer cicadas, as I left for my first dance. I won't sleep until you're home, she had called. So many layers of meaning. Even in such simple words. I shivered and turned the radio on, then the car heater. But I stayed cold.

Extremis

A man opened the door, looked her over and instantly knew, more or less, what had happened to her. 'Come in,' he said, taking her by the arm (his head turning as he scanned the street and the footpath) and leading her into the house.

His wife appeared in her nightie.

'Call the police,' he said to her. 'She's been attacked.'

Two little girls appeared, also in nighties.

'Go back to bed!' the wife said. 'Stay there.'

'Who's she?' one of them asked.

'She's in trouble,' said the man, 'and we're helping her. Go to bed!'

They obeyed.

The man said, 'Come and sit in the kitchen. Make strong tea with sugar,' he instructed his wife. 'Lots of sugar. That's what they say.'

But then, as he helped her up the hall to the kitchen, they passed a mirror. She saw herself for the first time in two weeks. Her mouth was bloodied and torn, one of her eyes was a pulpy mess, her throat was covered in purple and yellow bruises and the gaze that met her own was that of a stranger. Out-of-body experience.

At some stage, walking through the bush after she escaped the underground room, she thought about the nightmare of a trial. He wanted her to suffer and she had suffered but she hadn't died. On her nightdress and all over that bunker was the DNA that would put him away for life. She was exhibit A. Her suffering was exhibit A. What she always remembered afterwards, though, was the fierce, cold glitter of the stars in the night sky as she walked away from the bunker. She had never realised before how cold they were. How alien. The universe and life on earth had been revealed as a series of random events. The order we imposed on chaos was all our own idea and had nothing to do with the real state of play. Oddly, the realisation only strengthened her belief in the law. What else was there?

Two weeks earlier

She came out of the coffee shop laughing. That's probably why he noticed her. He resented happy women. A happy woman needed to be put in her place. She needed to face facts.

Fact 1. She's a woman. What has she got to be happy about?

Fact 2. She can't defend herself. Laughing in the street indicates confidence. Misplaced confidence. She needs to be taught.

Fact 3. A laughing woman might even be laughing at *him*. Which was, of course, intolerable.

Later on, she researched him. He had the usual childhood: single mother on drugs, sexually abused, beaten by various 'fathers', spent time in foster homes. He didn't hate women for no reason. He had his reasons. Plenty of them. But, essentially, she was in the wrong place at the wrong time. Once he set eyes on her, coming out of the coffee shop laughing, all fresh, blonde and happy (happy, the one thing they never taught him), he started stalking her. All kinds of things happened at this time that only made sense when the police explained it to her later. Not that anyone could really explain it. He was the dark side, the flip side of her life. She had been a loved child in a relatively stable family. That was why she was targeted for destruction. The fact that she had been loved showed on her face. It was there in her smile, in her laugh. The unloved often hate the loved. Besides which, he had taken violence in with his mother's milk.

He wasn't bad-looking but he had a twitchy, angry manner and he didn't wash. He didn't work, either, because like his mother and his siblings he had a drug problem. Drugs are expensive, as are most black market goods, so he had an extensive criminal record. Mostly so-called petty crimes, but there was one charge of aggravated assault. His victim was female. Of course. He had been in and out of jail for a few years now, so he had ample opportunities to do his own form of research.

That was how he came to obtain the black hood and the handcuffs. Jail being the poor and dysfunctional person's version of university. They all swapped stories and passed on tips inside. He wanted revenge on the world, especially the female sector of it, and the guys were very helpful. They were the ones who advised him to buy tranquillisers and sleeping tablets. To avoid complications. He did. The doctor was very sympathetic about his insomnia and bad nerves but the tablets would be put to a use he couldn't have imagined.

Her advantages trumped his disadvantages in the end, though. She understood him in a way he could never understand her. He possessed brute strength and cunning but, in the end, luckily for her, it wasn't enough. The guys had advised him to kill her after a couple of days because after that it got dangerous. But he was having too much fun.

She went to bed the night it happened with no sense of foreboding. She had just spent a day out with some friends at the beach and then they had a wonderful meal at a restaurant right on the water. It was one of those evenings where everything was perfect. In captivity, she would recall each detail to sustain herself. The little boats strung with lights reflecting on the water and the reproduction gondola, complete with gondolier in striped T-shirt, which had glided up to a jetty and dropped off diners in lovely clothes. The beautiful food (spanner crab spaghettini and lemon and lime soufflé – so perfect that it didn't look real), the wait staff in their black shorts and tops and long white aprons. In the dark where he had chained her up, she recalled all of this as if it was part of a mythical world of light and companionship. A dream to dream in the middle of a nightmare. She remembered all kinds of things from her childhood too. At that time, she wasn't aware of what he remembered from his childhood. Perhaps that was fortunate.

Her parents were overseas and she had broken up with her boyfriend a few months before. Her only sibling, Daniel, had died in a car crash twelve months before. She had just started a four-week holiday, so she wasn't expected at work either. Did her abductor know all this? Whether he knew it or not, it all played into his hands. This conjunction of facts meant that days went by after he abducted her with no one the wiser.

By the time she was reported missing, by a friend who called around to her flat and didn't like the chaotically messed-up bedroom she saw through the window, the trail had gone cold. By that time, she was in the bunker – down an old mine shaft – in darkness, handcuffed to a bed and being raped and beaten; completely at the mercy of an angry, smelly male who absolutely hated her for no reason she could understand.

For the first day, she was in shock and cried constantly. This made him beat her all the more and she soon learned not to cry no matter how she felt. Later she realised that it had taken a mere twenty-four hours for her to adopt the thinking and the body language of a battered wife. Don't make him angry. Don't argue. Don't look him in the eye. Obey. Submit.

But shock wears off and anger kicks in soon enough. She had to hide it completely, but it was there and it probably saved her life. It made her cold and cunning. It was cunning that helped her find the right tone of voice, respectful but not servile, in which to speak to him. It was a neutral, reasonable voice that she remembered from school. A female science teacher had had this voice: cool but not hostile. Any display of emotion set him off and she knew he could very easily beat her to death in a frenzy. He even told her one day that he would, of course, have to kill her. She could identify him. He had no choice. To him she was a sexed-up knock-'em toy and completely expendable.

Her existence became a matter of surviving that day with no thought for tomorrow. At night, he chained her up and went out. Temporarily safe, she cried and tried to make a plan. She found she could see quite well in the dark. In one corner was a Portaloo. Something that had horrified her when she first saw it. It was evidence that it had all been planned. And that was just plain crazy. The timber walls of the shaft had cartons of cigarettes stacked against them on one side and cartons of beer stacked against the wall near the double bed where she was chained. He needed no other entertainment. He had her. Another wall had canned goods and things like biscuits and fruit juice stacked up against it. Out in the middle of nowhere, underground and in the dark, she might as well have been drifting in space.

At night, if she looked up, through a gap in boards at the top of the shaft, she could see a patch of dark sky and a slice of the white sprinkle that was the Milky Way. Outside, the crickets made their music and sometimes she heard animals howling, grunting or screaming in terror as they were hunted and killed, probably by foxes or wild dogs. The indifference of the natural world was brought home to her in no uncertain terms. She was just another suffering, struggling form of life in the grand scheme of things. Strangely, this gave her comfort.

The night he came for her was like a military raid. He left nothing to chance. She woke to the overpowering smell of a chemical. It was chloroform. When she woke again, she was hooded and handcuffed and could feel that she was in a car, bumping over a road. When the car stopped, she heard a key turn in a lock and realised she was in the boot. He picked her up and carried her down, down. It seemed a very long way down. The hood was pulled off and she blinked in the light of a kerosene lamp, terror making her heart race and her mouth dry.

'What do you want?' she demanded.

He smacked her face. 'Shut up!' he yelled. He knew how important it was to get control immediately. The guys had been most insistent on that point. He tore her nightdress off and raped her. 'Slut!' he snarled. 'You don't ask me nothin'. Understand?'

She nodded. Then he started to beat her and mercifully she blacked out. After that, she was beaten almost every day. There was no rhyme or reason to it. That was just how it was.

Inevitably, he got careless. He took the handcuffs off after a few days. He started to forget little things. Like the bottle of chloroform left on top of the cartons of cigarettes. Of course he knew it could be used. But by her? Impossible. She was too stupid, too broken, and besides he was going to kill her soon. He told her so. She was looking ugly, he told her. Her bloodied eye and swollen face were becoming a turn-off.

Then one night he hauled a large tin tub out of one of the corners of the shaft. She assumed it had been hidden behind something ever since she had been there. He boiled some water on a gas hotplate and poured it in. He unchained her and ordered her to wash. She stank, he told her in disgust. She stood on trembling legs and walked to the tub. No need to undress since she had been naked ever since the first night he brought her there.

The warm water was lovely even though it made the numerous cuts and abrasions on her body sting. He tossed a bar of soap and a washer in and she washed herself, luxuriating in the experience in a surreal way. Then she remembered her mother bathing her as a child and felt tears in her eyes. She blinked them away at once. Crying in front of him was simply too dangerous. She heard him make his way to the top of the shaft on the ancient wooden stairs. Careless of him, but a relief for her since she had been convinced he would try to drown her. She hauled herself out of the tub and stumbled over to the bottle of chloroform. Quickly hiding it under the mattress, she stumbled back into the tub before he came back down. He didn't seem to notice the bottle was gone. If he did, he would beat her. Perhaps he would beat her to death.

'Get out of there! Dry yourself!' he said.

Did he sound suspicious? He looked angry but he always looked angry. She felt a bit more human after the bath and decided that while she felt that way she had to do something.

'I feel sick,' she said. 'I think I need to see a doctor.'

He smacked her over the head for that. She was a nuisance, he told her. Look at her. What use was she? She wasn't pretty any more, he complained. He pushed her over to the bed but only so he could put the chain back on her inflamed, lacerated and throbbing ankle.

Sitting on the bed, she slipped her hand under the mattress and her fingers found the chloroform bottle. But she was exhausted from lack of proper food and felt so weak she couldn't get the bottle out in time to do anything. Still, it had to be soon and it would take all her courage to attempt it.

Later, the police decided he made her take the bath to destroy evidence. To wash it away. Probably, they told her, that was the night he was going to kill her and leave her body down the shaft. Seal the entrance with rocks. No one would ever find her. That was his plan, anyway.

At some point that night, he took the chain off again. She would never really know why, but her guess was that he had decided to kill her and thought she was too weak and ill to fight back. Yes. He had become careless.

Sometime later, she was wandering semi-naked in the darkness beside a road wearing her torn and bloodstained nightdress. But she didn't know it. A truckie saw her and thought by the state she was in he should call the police. He didn't want to get involved. She was perfectly happy. She believed she was in the house with the nice man, his wife and their two little daughters. She could see them. They were speaking to her. The suppurating flesh around her ankle was badly infected. She was delirious and in a state of nervous shock and when the police picked her up, she waved to the family that had helped her. The policemen thought she was a psych patient on the run.

It was a day or so before they went to check the mineshaft. By then, someone had thought to put her name in a computer and saw she was a missing person. Two policemen climbed down the old stairs to the bottom of the shaft and found the body of a male. Wrapped around his neck was a bloodied chain and his head had been bashed in with a rock, also bloodied. Clearly the girl's story of the mad abductor was not simply some wild delusion. They were careful not to touch anything. Including the bottle of chloroform on the floor. Forensics arrived and set up a crime scene.

The two policemen couldn't get out of there fast enough.

'The bloody place's a torture chamber,' one of them said.

His colleague nodded. 'Weird. Never seen anything like it. She didn't look strong enough, did she? To do that?'

'Mad people are very strong.'

His colleague laughed. 'And you reckon he wasn't mad?'

'Barking bloody mad. He turned his back on a woman he'd tortured. Mistake.'

Gallows humour was their salvation. It surprised them all the more when she burst into tears after being told he was dead and that she had probably killed him.

'No. No,' she sobbed. 'I used the chloroform. I remember it! I couldn't kill anyone! I couldn't! I left him there…'

'No one blames you,' one of the policemen told her, shaking his head. Then looked guilty, as if he had said something he shouldn't.

The other one said, 'Well, I don't suppose he hit himself over the head.' Trying for humour.

None of it helped. She was inconsolable.

A few weeks later, her family doctor persuaded her to go to a male therapist, an energetic, sophisticated, elderly man with the faintest hint of an accent. For the therapist, life was divided into two zones. In the first zone, until he was four, he had no experience of evil, at least none that he could remember. In the second zone, after he was five, there was a world war and his mother died in a concentration camp. For him, this girl's journey to the heart of darkness was not the complicated thing it might be for others. Evil *was*. It simply was. His task was to mitigate its effects.

The girl came into his consulting room and sat there, pale and shattered and drugged. Tranquillisers. No make-up. Faint yellowish smudges on her skin were all that was left of the bruises. The cuts and lacerations had healed and the eye that had been a pulpy mess now displayed just the purple-yellowish remains of a black eye. Surgeons had saved the sight in that eye. The infected ankle now only had some small ulcers encircling it.

The consulting room was spotlessly clean but warm and bright with large windows, light walls and curtains, pine furniture and a big red rug on the floor.

After the formalities he told her, 'Now, begin at the beginning.'

She looked confused and frightened. 'What…is the beginning?'

'Ah,' he leaned back in his chair and he smiled. 'The beginning is anything you want it to be.' Slowly, cunningly, he would attempt to guide her back to confidence and autonomy.

She had thought he would pronounce her mad, prescribe different tablets and send her home. He checked the clock over the door with a discreet glance. Each session lasted an hour. It wasn't much, he knew, but he also knew, as she did not, that it marked the beginning of a dangerous and unpredictable journey.

He sat forward and smiled again. 'The beginning?' he said.

'He didn't even know my name,' she began to cry. 'Some days I ask myself how he could want to do those things to me, even kill me, when he didn't even know my name.'

He could have said, 'Of course, that is the nature of war. Necessarily, you kill people whose names you don't know, who have done nothing to you.'

But it would have been self-indulgent to go down that road. It would have been like showing off.

'The beginning?' he said and smiled, so they could both be brave.

Finch Street

The whisky gleamed. It sparkled in the bottle. It was like a jewel, sitting up on the shelf. He had bought it to test himself and he hadn't touched a drink for twelve months. I'll buy it just to prove to myself that I'm cured. That was the mistake he had made so many times in the past, but he told himself that he was not ready then. An alcoholic is never cured, he knew that. Whisky had always seemed to him to be a real man's drink. He knew the truth, though. There was nothing heroic about being a drunk.

His wife had tired of cleaning him up. Of finding and emptying the bottles he hid all over the house and even the yard. Thinking about this only made the bottle on the shelf fill his mind all the more. It filled his mind until there wasn't room for anything else. He knew he had a thirst that could never be quenched; one drink was too much and a million drinks weren't enough. The familiar ache started in the pit of his stomach and went slowly up to find its place in the part of his brain that made him a drunk.

After work, he drove around in circles, slowly moving closer to his house with each turn of the wheel. Afraid of what he would do when he got there. The front door opened on a silent, empty house that seemed airless. He walked to the shelf where the bottle was and as he stood there he thought about his wife, his children, the job he used to have. A much better job than the one he had now. He took the bottle down and held it in his hands while he looked into its gold-brown depths. He felt as if he was trapped in the bottle, like one of those miniature ships. Uncapping it, he walked into the kitchen and when he reached the sink and looked at the glasses, he ached to drink. It was almost a physical pain. Then the cuckoo clock chimed and it was as if a voice was telling him he was cuckoo, cuckoo, cuckoo. Savagely, he upended the bottle and poured the whisky down the sink. He watched it drain away like brown blood. He was covered in sweat. His hands trembled as he rinsed the sink.

Picking up his car keys, he walked to the door, forcing himself not to run. He wasn't cured and he never would be. The only cure was never to drink again. He looked back through the house to where he could see the empty bottle on the sink. He smiled to himself as he closed the front door. It was that day's victory. One day at a time.

Martin McConnell opened his eyes and sat up in bed. His pyjamas were soaked in sweat. It was the dream again. The one he always had. It wasn't such a frightening dream, what he could remember of it. It even had a happy ending. He smiled to himself. Yet it terrified him. He always woke up soaked in sweat, his heart racing. The funny part was he didn't even drink. Never had. He had never been married either and he had no children, yet everything in the dream was so familiar. Even the house, though he owned no house. He had lived at home with his parents ever since he had been involved in a near fatal car accident. He had no memory of anything before the accident. He had been in a coma for months in a private clinic and the part of his brain where memory functioned had been badly damaged. His parents had told him all of this.

He looked up and saw his mother standing in the doorway watching him.

'Are you all right, Martin?' Her face was tense and she was frowning. She always worried about him. He had been a late baby and she was overprotective.

'I'm fine. I had a strange dream, that's all,' he smiled at her.

She was a striking-looking woman with thick white hair and piercing blue eyes. Not tall but, even at seventy-two, she had an imposing presence. His father, a scientist, had died two years before. He didn't tell her that he had started having this dream a few days after his father died or that he had it regularly.

'I've made some coffee,' his mother said, looking relieved. 'And some French toast. Come and have breakfast with me. I've set the table out on the deck.'

'Okay. I'll have a shower first. That dream made me sweat,' he laughed.

She closed the door and soon he heard her clinking cups down the hall.

There were no towels in the bathroom, so he walked up the hall to the linen cupboard and took a couple out. Looking up, he saw a photo album on top of the linen cupboard that looked as if it was just about to fall. There were several photo albums up there. Sometimes he teased his mother that he must have been the most photographed child on the planet.

'Your father was the shutterbug, not me. If you have to blame someone, blame him,' his mother told him.

He took the album down and reached up to put it back on top of the others. Then he looked at the cover. He couldn't remember ever seeing this album before. When he opened it, a photo that had obviously been lying loose inside fell out on to the floor. It was a photo of a house. There was a woman standing in front of the house, smiling. She was wearing a white dress with shoulder straps and she was holding a baby in her arms. He turned the photo over and saw written on the back, 'Natalie with Jamie, the house in Finch Street, 1979.' He knew this woman, though he had no idea who she was or how he knew her. He recognised her face, but the baby was simply a white bundle. This was the kind of photo people took when a woman arrived home from hospital with a new baby and as he stared at it he knew that was exactly what it was. Finch Street. The name stirred something in the depths of memory. Something that had been sleeping began to wake. He was bewildered. The house, as he could clearly see, was the one he had been dreaming about on and off for several years now. The one where he poured the whisky down the sink. He was suddenly terribly frightened. He thought he was going mad so he put the photo back in the album and threw it up on to the top of the cupboard.

His mother appeared at the end of the hall. 'Martin? Have you had your shower?'

'I'll have it after breakfast. I was looking for towels…'

'Well, come on then. The coffee will get cold,' she laughed.

He followed her through the kitchen and out on to the deck. It was going to be a beautiful day, fine and warm with just a faint breeze.

His mother poured the coffee and the smell made him hungry. She handed his plate across the table and he ate a piece of French toast.

'Nice and crispy?' his mother said, opening the paper.

That was how he liked French toast.

His mother pointed down into the garden. 'See the camellias? Don't they look wonderful?'

Martin forced his mind back to the present. Back to reality. 'Umm,' he nodded sipping his coffee, 'wonderful.'

She smiled, 'You seem a bit vague, darling,' she said, going back to her paper.

'It's that dream,' he said. 'I can't shake it off.'

'Dreams are just dreams. They're sort of fantasies. It'll fade.'

He thought about the photo in the album and the house. The woman. The baby. What did it mean?

It was a Sunday and his mother played bridge on Sundays, so he drove her over to the house where bridge was played. The woman who lived there was called Muriel or Miriam or something. His mother waved and he waved back.

Driving down to the corner, he knew he had to turn right but he made his decision and turned left instead. He had looked Finch Street up in the street directory. He had to know if the house was real. Perhaps it was all just some bizarre coincidence. Filled with a mixture of apprehension and burning curiosity, he turned into Fuchsia Drive and changed lanes just in time to avoid a collision with a four-wheel drive. Loud curses screamed out of a car window followed him as he sped away from the large blue and silver vehicle. Four-wheel drives belonged in the bush, he thought angrily, though he snorted with laughter when he remembered the driver's puce face and his open mouth gone square with fury.

Finch Street, when he found it, was a quiet street. No thoroughfare. He looked at the street and knew it was all wrong. The houses in the photo were old. Federation most of them. This Finch Street was brand-new. Some of the houses still had the builder's signs in the yard. It was one of those designer streets with fancy pavers laid down instead of bitumen. It wasn't the same street. He pulled over and took out the street directory. There was no other Finch Street. Disappointment.

He sat thinking for a while, watching children on bikes and rollerblades and fathers watering the new and struggling lawns. The Finch Street in the photo was in another city and he didn't know which one but not finding it had somehow solidified the house, the street, the woman and the baby in his mind. They existed. He was sure of it.

His mother wouldn't have to be picked up until the afternoon, so he drove home and took down one of the photo albums. Then he decided to take down all the photo albums and look at all of them. He opened the unfamiliar one. Its cover was patterned in what he thought was called paisley. He had read somewhere that paisley was very popular in the sixties, or was it the seventies? He took out the photo of the woman in the white dress and held it in his hand. Who are you? How do I know you? Why are you so familiar? Her pretty face stared at him out of the photo. She was as mysterious and haunting to him as the Sphinx. She was blonde and had a neat, symmetrical face and very blue eyes.

Thinking about the Sphinx led him to thoughts of ancient Egypt and the afterlife and from there to reincarnation. Was that it? Was she from a former life? No, that was crazy. And why would his mother have her photo?

He flipped open another album, one he was familiar with. His mother had often looked at it with him. She loved looking at photos of him as a child. He studied the little blonde boy that had become him and as he stared he became aware that not all the photos were the same. There were subtle differences. The clothes, for example, were from different decades. He could see that quite clearly now, although he had never noticed it before. The backgrounds too were different, even though his mother claimed they had never lived in any other house but the one they now had. The one he had grown up in. They had spent five years in another house, where they had lived early in their marriage, but he wouldn't have been born then. His father, he knew, had been a lecturer in science at one of the universities in Melbourne. There was even a difference in coloration in the photos. Some of the photos were the product of an older development process, as he could now see quite clearly, but in the photos the little blond boys were identical. What could it mean?

Then, just like that, he turned a page of the paisley-covered album and was confronted with the fact that things were very much stranger than he had ever imagined. There he stood on his wedding day, smiling proudly, arm in arm with the woman from the other photo; the one photographed with a baby in her arms. His mouth went dry. He couldn't swallow. Was it an older brother? One he had never been told about? Was it some relative who had an uncanny resemblance to him? Over to the side in the photo was a street that ran near the church. And a side view of a tram. Only two cities had trams running in the seventies and one of them was Melbourne.

His hands were shaking as he threw the albums back up on top of the cupboard. He couldn't look at the photos any more. Not just now. He would have to later but not now. He went into the kitchen and put some eggs on to boil, put some toast in the toaster and opened a can of soup. That was the extent of his cooking abilities. His mother did everything for him. Always had. He sat at the table and ate in the silent house until he could bear it no more. Then he turned on the radio and let techno music roar through the house. Anything was better than listening to his own thoughts.

Later, he decided to have a sleep but as soon as he fell asleep he started to dream. In the dream, his wife came in with a glass of fruit juice in her hand and gave it to him. He knew at once that this was not the house in Finch Street but some other place. His wife looked tired, her mouth set and sullen.

'I'm glad you're being sensible,' she said as he drained the glass. "I don't want you falling down drunk at Annie's school concert. We'd better go if we're going to drop Jamie at Mum's. We're going to be late. I'd better phone her."

He didn't answer. He knew that if he did it would end in an argument. As it always did.

She dressed his son Jamie while he went to get his car keys from the hall but when he stepped into the hall he found it had disappeared. In its place was an endless wilderness and, looming over it, a towering mountain, black and shrouded in mist. From the top of it, a huge eagle flew at him. He ran but couldn't move. His feet could find no traction and when he tried to scream he had no voice. The eagle attacked him, tearing at his body while his mouth opened and closed and no sound came out. He turned his head and saw his wife and son watching from the door. Their faces had no expression. He was dying but neither of them gave any sign that anything was wrong. He looked into the eagle's eyes as it tore at him. They were his father's eyes.

He sat up in bed, shaking and sweating. He put his hand to his forehead. He didn't have a temperature and yet he felt fevered. Delirious. His wife in the dream had had the face of the woman in the photo. He put his own face in his hands. 1979. He hadn't even been born until 1981. Was he going mad? Should he see a doctor?

His mother had always called him a miracle baby because he was born when she was forty-two. 'The doctor couldn't believe it. He told me it was impossible. That I must be mistaken when I told him I was sure I was pregnant. But I was. Then he tried to convince me that there would be something wrong with the baby. When you were born, I said to him "Look, he's perfect. Absolutely perfect." And you were.'

It was easy to see why she had become overprotective.

He had to find Finch Street. He had to find that house. He would have to go back to the photo album and try to find a clue as to where it was but he couldn't discuss any of this with his mother. It would worry her and she would probably want him to see a psychotherapist. He had become convinced that if he could just find the house and see that it was real the dreams would go away. He had some connection with that house and if he could only find out what it was his problem would be solved.

That afternoon when he picked his mother up, he must have looked as strange as he felt, because she suddenly said, 'Are you all right, darling? You look pale and you haven't said a word.'

He blinked, trying to clear his head. 'I'm okay. I'm not sleeping all that well at the moment.'

She was all tenderness and concern in an instant. 'I'll make you some camomile tea with honey as soon as we get home,' she said and patted his arm.

He didn't really understand himself why he was being so secretive. Some memory stirred and was lost again. He had decided that his mother had either forgotten about the paisley-covered album or didn't know about it for some reason. He would take it down when he got home and move it to a safe place. He felt for some reason that she would have destroyed it if she knew about it. It upset him that he felt this way. Eventually he would have to tell her but not yet. First he would go to Melbourne and find Finch Street so he could uncover whatever secrets were hidden there. It was either that or go slowly insane.

His mother wouldn't want him to go to Melbourne on his own. She didn't like him to drive long distances either. She still treated him like the teenager he had been when he had the car crash. 'You'll never be the same again. The doctor said you were lucky to survive. They said your memory could come back bit by bit. They told me to give up on you but I wouldn't.'

She had told him this so many times he knew it word for word. That was why he never played contact sports or went clubbing with his friends. His mother couldn't bear for him to take any risks with himself at all. What could he say? She had told him so many times how she had sat by his hospital bed and talked to him and played his favourite songs on a Walkman, putting the earphones on his ears, while the doctors looked at her pityingly and waited for him to die. Three or four times they suggested that she should consider turning off the life support machine. She always refused, even threatening to get a court order on one occasion. Through the power of love and sheer willpower, she had brought him back from the dead. He could never forget that. He had girlfriends from time to time but most of them gave up after they met his mother. They knew what they were up against and wisely withdrew. Martin didn't blame his mother for the way she was. He knew she couldn't help it.

Luckily, one of the boys Martin played chess with sometimes, Gary Tutin, was involved in some kind of long-distance romance with a girl who sang in a rock band in Melbourne and he was happy to make the bus trip with him. Once the bus rolled into the transit centre in Melbourne, they went their separate ways.

'I'll see you here tomorrow at three-thirty p.m. The bus goes at four,' he told Gary, who was a bit of a wild lad with hair that was mostly peroxide blond except for where it was green from swimming in a chlorinated pool once too often. Things like this were always happening to Gary. They were opposites and, as often happens, got along extremely well.

'Yeah, see ya, man,' Gary said. 'Pow!' Pretending to shoot him with his finger he was gone.

Martin had no certainty that he would see him at all, or at least not at the appointed hour. If he didn't turn up, Martin would board the bus without him. He knew that if he wasn't back in Sydney exactly when he said he would be, his mother would fall apart. He had seen her do that on numerous occasions and it was very unpleasant for everybody concerned and best avoided if possible. He didn't like to worry her, anyway. It made him feel as if he had failed her somehow.

Martin caught a cab from the transit centre to a motel, checked in and fell asleep on the single bed. He drew the curtains to make the room dark because the bus trip had exhausted him, but he knew he wouldn't sleep if he could see any light. The windows of the motel room looked out on to a swimming pool full of bright, blue water. The pool was deserted but a candy-striped beach ball was floating in it. Melbourne was still too cold for swimming, even though it was officially the beginning of spring, but some hardy souls (probably children) had been in the pool.

Lying down in the darkened room, he fell asleep within seconds. He dreamed he was in a speeding car hurtling down a tunnel and the lights on the roof of the tunnel were passing his eyes at such a rate that they turned into pinwheels of light. For some reason, he was looking up at them through the windscreen and when he looked at his hands gripping the steering wheel, he knew something was wrong. The steering wheel wouldn't turn. He held on to it even though he knew it was no good. It wouldn't steer the car and yet the car went straight ahead as if it knew where it had to take him. He felt a strong sense of peace as he realised that it was not his responsibility any more.

Then he saw the woman in the white dress standing in the middle of the tunnel with the baby in her arms. She held it out to him; he was going to hit her. He thought, the baby will be killed, and he started to scream. When he tried to take his hands off the wheel, they were stuck. He knew he was going to die but there was nothing he could do. When the car hit the woman and the baby, they turned into smoke. Smoke and mirrors, he thought, and then he woke up.

He was shivering. The sun had gone down and the air conditioning had chilled the room. He stumbled as he got off the bed to adjust the air conditioning and caught sight of his face in the mirror over the basin. The trouble was, it wasn't his face but the face of an older man. It was him when he was about thirty years old. Fleetingly, he felt a scream rising in his throat and panic beating at his brain. He choked the panic off and took a deep breath, splashed water on his face and looked in the mirror again. He looked a bit haunted but otherwise quite normal. He adjusted the air conditioning. Tiredness and hunger (he hadn't eaten for hours) were playing tricks on him and he decided to go and eat in the motel dining room.

Tomorrow he would find Finch Street. Soon, he hoped, the nightmares would end. The truth might set him free. He recognised the tunnel from his dream. It was the one they had gone through on a summer's day, in his friend's little green car, laughing and shouting with music playing very loud, just before another car crossed the median strip and spun them off the road. It was the day after his sixteenth birthday. He wouldn't think about that now. He still had the night to get through.

The pretty, brown-haired girl on the reception desk gave him a sweet, professional smile. She was as sleek and neat as a pedigree cat and her eyes were an arresting shade. Almost amethyst. She had a lucky mouth. One that looked as if it was smiling, even in repose. He had read somewhere that the Chinese said that was lucky. She found him attractive; her arresting eyes told him so.

'The dining room is to your right, sir. You're just in time for dinner,' she told him with a look that suggested this was definite proof of genius.

'Thank you,' Martin smiled.

'You're welcome.'

Better professional politeness than surly coldness. Or was it? He couldn't decide.

The dining room looked out on to a garden which featured large green shrubs and some white hibiscus, lit by spot lighting. Traffic moved along bumper to bumper. The tail end of the rush hour.

He had a steak and some overcooked vegetables and a glass dish of ice cream. He drank a beer because he thought it might make him sleep. It didn't go with the ice cream and made him slightly sick but back in his room he found it easy to sleep.

He didn't dream this time. Just after the car crash that had almost killed him, his mother had made him promise not to drink alcohol. His friend, the driver, had had two beers before the crash but Martin had been completely sober. He didn't really care for alcohol.

Next morning, he set off quite early to find Finch Street. He did it without great difficulty. His mother always said he had inherited his father's sense of direction. Hers was virtually non-existent. He had a small backpack with him and in it he had a photo of the woman and the baby, in front of the house he was looking for. That made finding the house very easy. There it was, almost unchanged. A different fence but the same red-brick house as in the photo he held in his hand. As he stood there looking at the house, a girl carrying plastic shopping bags full of groceries came up the street.

She gave him a funny look, as if she thought she might know him, then she said, very politely, 'Are you lost? Looking for a street?'

'No, I was looking for this house,' he said. 'Do you know the name of the people who live here?'

'I live here,' she said, warily. 'Are you selling something?'

Then he really looked at her for the first time and his head swam. He had to blink to clear it. She was so like the woman in the white dress it was uncanny. She could almost be her twin but she was too young. Then he noticed her looking at the photo in his hand.

'Where did you get that?' she said, quite sharply.

'I found it in a photo album.'

'Who are you? Are we related?'

The question stunned him. What could he say? 'We might be,' he said uncertainly. 'Do you know the woman in this photo?'

'That's my mother and that would be my older brother Jamie she's holding. I have a photo just like it.'

Excitement made his heart race. 'Do you know where I can find them?'

'You can find them in the cemetery,' she said, rather bitterly. 'They both died in a car crash. Before I was born.'

'Before you were…'

'Who are you?' she said again, staring into his eyes.

'Let me introduce myself.' He smiled. 'My name is Martin. This photo was in an album in my mother's house in Sydney.'

She considered him closely for a while then she said, 'Come in.'

On the bus on the way back, Gary was hyped up and wanted to tell him all about his adventures with his girlfriend but all Martin wanted to do was sleep. He needed to escape from all the questions that were racing through his mind but Gary talked and talked.

The girl (her name was Marielle) had told Martin a terrible story. Her father had been an alcoholic and her parents were separated. One day after he had drunk a whole bottle of whisky, he picked her mother and her brother up to drive them to a cousin's school concert. Her mother didn't have a car. He was one of those people who never seemed drunk. Like a lot of alcoholics. Her mother had been eight months pregnant with her and she had only found out she was pregnant after she decided to end the marriage. They were running late for the concert; her mother had told her grandmother so on the phone just before they left. On the way there, her drunken father had crashed into an electricity pole.

'My father was living in this house at the time of the crash. My mother had moved into a flat. That's how my grandparents knew about the whisky. My grandparents actually own this house and they had rented it to my parents so they had a key. They came here after the crash to clean up before some tenants moved in and found the empty bottle sitting on the sink. It must have been a terrible moment.'

Her father and her brother had died but her mother had lived long enough to be put on life support. They kept her on life support until Marielle could be delivered. 1980. She was a year older than he was. Her grandparents had brought her up and now she was back in the house in Finch Street and studying at university. She shared the house with two other students. Her grandparents had rented it out for years but had never sold it.

'Do you have any photos of your father?' he had asked her.

She looked at him as if this was a stupid question. 'Can you imagine how bitter they were? He killed their daughter and their grandson and if it wasn't for technology, I'd be dead too. They burned every photo of him and only kept the ones of my mother and my brother. I was never allowed to ask questions about him. Once my grandmother was talking to my grandfather about how glad she had been that they were getting divorced. "But he still managed to kill my sweet Jamie," I heard her saying. She wouldn't talk about him. It was as if he had never existed. Anything I know about the crash I have from my grandfather. I don't own a single photo of my father.'

'So you don't even know what he looked like?'

'Not a clue. I can see some things about myself that are not like my mother so I suppose they must be like him, but that's not the same as knowing, is it?'

'What was his name?'

'It's funny,' she said laughing. 'It was the same as yours. Martin.'

'And the surname?'

'McConnell.'

Eventually he did fall asleep on the bus and he dreamed he was back in the house in Finch Street again, standing at the sink. As usual. When the man at the sink turned around, though, it wasn't him. This time it was the man with the face he had seen in the mirror in the motel room. Him and not him. Him at thirty. The man in the dream looked straight at him and then picked up the bottle of whisky and poured it down the sink.

When Martin woke up on the bus, disoriented and head still buzzing with fatigue, he thought he understood. Not everything. Not the most important thing but some of it was starting to make a weird kind of sense. Like the fact that his father had been a geneticist. A brilliant one, according to his mother. Then as he looked out the window of the bus watching the scenery fly past, the thought came to him out of nowhere: if he hadn't had a drink in twelve months, a whole bottle of whisky would have knocked him out. It might even have killed him. Alcohol poisoning.

Martin paid the cab driver and walked up to the front gate feeling a kind of finality. Now there would be no more secrets. He smiled to himself. Families and secrets seemed to go together. Without their secrets, how could they live with each other? Now, though, he had to know. Time for the truth.

He opened the gate and looked up to see his mother watching him. She didn't wave. She just watched him all the way to the front door, which was unlocked, because she was expecting him. He went in. His mother had come inside too and was sitting in her favourite light blue armchair with her back to a large picture window. Through it, he could see the camellias she loved so much.

'How was your trip?" she said brightly, but he picked up the undertone of suspicion.

Of course that could have been paranoia but if what he suspected was true, he had a right to be paranoid and she had a right to be suspicious. He took his backpack off and put it on the floor.

'The young travel so lightly,' she said. She disapproved of travelling lightly. 'When I was twenty, I went to Europe with my parents. I took five suitcases and I came back with six!' She smiled her enchanting smile.

Even though his mind was on weighty, even frightening, matters, he smiled back. His mother could be irresistibly charming when she wanted to be. He opened his backpack and took out the paisley-covered photo album and when she saw it all the colour drained from her face and for the first time since he had known her she looked her age.

'Where did you find that?' she asked him, coldly.

'It was up on top of the linen cupboard with all the other albums. I suppose you just forgot about it. When I was a child it wouldn't have seemed important and I suppose grief made you want to keep it. After that, you just forgot. When I was in Melbourne, I went to Finch Street. I met a girl named Marielle. Your granddaughter, I believe.'

She folded her hands in her lap in a gesture of resignation. 'So, you've worked it out have you?' she said, softly and sadly. 'I hoped you would never have to know.'

'I think I've worked it out. Tell me if I've got it right. In 1980, the first Martin McConnell, an alcoholic and also your son, was killed in a car crash in Melbourne. How am I doing so far?'

His mother nodded. 'Go on,' she said.

'You were overwhelmed with grief when he died…'

'I was suicidal,' she corrected him, in a monotone.

'Okay. You were suicidal but what could be done?'

'That's why your father decided to do it, you see? He thought he was going to lose both of us – Martin and me.'

'And he was a geneticist, wasn't he? He knew just what to do. He knew how to give you back your son.'

'It was a gift of love, Martin. Can you understand? Your father had all the papers on cloning. He knew it had been attempted – successfully. The scientist involved had destroyed the experiment but we knew it was possible. He obtained the DNA from a lock of your baby hair I kept in a box and he created an embryo. The pregnancy was perfectly normal, no different to my first one, but we worried that at my age questions might be asked, so he left his lecturing position at the university and we moved to Sydney. Your birth was joyous for your father and for me but when you almost died in a car crash too, I began to believe it was your destiny. Only for the first day after the crash, though. After that, I decided to fight and I won. We won.'

'So I'm a clone. A carbon copy of the first Martin McConnell.'

'Yes, darling, that's right,' she said in such a reasonable tone of voice that he felt like shaking her.

'And who does that make me? Who am I? I'm a dead man. I'm a year younger than my own daughter. I'm a freak.'

'Don't be angry, darling. I did it because I couldn't bear to lose you.' She sounded distraught. He had never been angry with her before. 'It's just as if you were an identical twin,' she said in a soothing voice.

'Identical twins have different fingerprints. Mine are exactly the same as his and he's dead, so who does that make me?'

'You're my son, darling.'

'Your son is dead.'

'Martin, don't say that.' She put her hand over her mouth as if she wished she had never spoken.

He almost wished she hadn't spoken too, but at the same time he knew it had to be. At least now he knew he wasn't mad. 'He wasn't drunk when the car crashed, you know. He poured that bottle of whisky down the sink. It was the steering on the car. It failed or it locked and he couldn't control the car.'

'How do you know?' She looked doubtful but pleased. She wanted to believe him.

He looked straight at her. 'Who would know better than me?' He put his backpack on.

'What are you doing? Where are you going?'

'I'm moving in with Gary for a while. I asked him on the bus. I need time to think.'

'You can think here, can't you?' She had tears in her eyes.

'I'll come and see you on the weekend, I promise. It's time I did something about getting my own place,' he said in a deliberately casual tone of voice. He had seen her have hysterics and he didn't believe he could handle that.

'What about clothes?' she said, wiping her eyes.

'I'll get some on the weekend,' he told her.

She walked to the door with him, kissed his cheek, stood on the deck and waved as he got in his car.

But when he stopped the car in the driveway, waiting for a break in the traffic, he heard the hideous sound of her sobbing and wailing his name over and over again inside the house. He found her almost frightening now. It wasn't that he didn't love her. He loved her and he would come back as he had promised but now he had to find out who he was and that was something he had to do on his own. He didn't think he had done it in his previous life. He was twice-born. How many people get two bites of the cherry? He had already wasted one life and he wasn't going to let it happen again. He accelerated smoothly out into the street and joined the line of cars heading for the highway.

About the Author

Antonia Hildebrand is a poet, short story writer and essayist. She was born and educated in Toowoomba, Queensland. After her marriage to Reinhard Hildebrand, she moved with him to Hamburg, Germany. She lived and worked in Europe for three years and also travelled in Europe and Asia before returning to Australia. She then studied at the Toowoomba Technical College, going to evening classes before gaining admission to the University of Queensland. She graduated Bachelor of Arts in 1987 with majors in both German and English literature. In 1993 she graduated Master of Letters (German) from the University of New England.

Her first published short story, 'Nothing Ever Happens', appeared in *Woman's Day* in 1981 and *Downs Images* in 1982 and she has since been widely published in journals, magazines and anthologies in Australia as well as Britain and the USA.

Her poems have appeared in *Coppertales, Iodine Poetry Journal* USA, *Poetrix, Harvester* and *Squidink*. Her short stories have appeared in *Downs Images, Woman's Day, Shortz, First Edition Magazine, Tirra Lirra* and *Four W Seventeen*.

An essay on John Howard, 'Ordinary Australians', was published in *Overland* in 2003.

In 1998 she won the University of Southern Queensland Library Poetry Prize and in 1999 the Fellowship of Australian Writers' Marjorie Barnard Short Story Award.

In 2002 she began contributing to Radio National's *Bush Telegraph* program. Many of her short stories have been broadcast by *Queensland Storyteller* on Radio 4RPH and by *Words and Music* on Radio 91.3 FM. Her Radio National pieces and her film reviews and essays were collected for her book *The Past is Another Country: Viewpoints, Essays & Reviews*, published in 2003. She has also explored growing to adulthood, living in Europe and returning to Australia in her memoir *Beautiful Life*. In 2004 she co-wrote, with John Boshammer, *Boshy and Me* – a biography of his rugby legend father, Kev Boshammer. A poetry collection, *The Sweet Time*, was published in 2006. Her most recent book, *The Blind Colossus*, was published by Ginninderra Press in 2015. Her next book, *Underclass/Overclass: Twenty Essays on Oppression*, is a work in progress.